Diamond

KIARRA THE DON

This is a work of fiction. It is not meant to depict, portray, or represent any particular real persons. All the characters, incidents, and dialogues are the products of the author's imagination and are not to be constructed as real. Any resemblance to actual events or persons living or dead, is purely coincidental.

ISBN
9798853543140

COVER ART BY
@KiarraTheDon (Instagram)

FIRST EDITION
Printed in the United States of America

Copyright © 2024 by Kiarra Boulware. All rights reserved. No part of this book may be reproduced in any form without permission from the author, except by reviewer who may quote passages to be printed in a newspaper or magazine.

This Book Is Dedicated To

Tamauri Khalil Boulware

Sometimes, things happen long before your brain is able to understand why. Though I miss you more than my heart can bear, my only regret is spending more time questioning God about your absence than actually mourning you. I've learned through my own process that grieving doesn't mean that I have to live without you. In fact, it means the opposite, as I am learning to live with you in spiritual form. I miss you and I love you. I needed you, but God needed you more.

Brooklynn Sade' Norman

You are the reason that I can dream. Every goal I set forth for myself thus far, I have accomplished effortlessly because you are my motivation. I love you and I pray for you more than I do myself. After consistent heartbreak, trauma, tragedy, and despair, your entry into this world made my life worth living again. There is no measure to the lengths I will go to make you smile. You have saved me from myself time again, and I will spend the rest of my life – and yours – making sure you feel loved, cared for, happy, healthy, protected, and provided for.

Grandma Mona (My Saving Grace)

They say, 'There's no love like a mother's love.' I say they must have never been loved by their grandmother. When the world turned their back on me, you stayed ten toes down with me and loved me in spite of myself. The sacrifices you have made for me are not in vain. I am everything I am because of your prayers, caretaking, and compassion. For everything you have done and been for me, I am forever indebted. I look forward to the days when the roles reverse, and I can take care of you how you deserve.

"Comrade Boo"

Brother, there is a hole in my heart that you took with your physical presence. I miss everything about you – your smile, your laugh, your corny jokes, your stiff dance moves, your listening ear, your great advice, your protection, your comfort, your tough love (only sometimes because we all know that you were really tender when it comes to me), but most of all, your loyalty. You loved me like we came out of the same womb, and I am extremely grateful to have experienced a love such as yours. Thank you for pushing me to embrace my gift as a writer. Watch how I go up for us.
#LLTG Carry On I Shall.

"Argie"

Never will I question God, but I do wish there was a way to rewind the hands of time. You were so full of life and I just knew I had more time with you. I needed more time with you. It was such an honor to be not only your sister, but your friend. You were so selfless, kind, caring, nonjudgemental, sassy, funny, and full of life. Thank you for keeping my secrets. I will always honor the pivotal role you played in my life.

To All The Girls Like Me

Have you spent years looking for love in the wrong places? Don't worry; me too. May we find the love in ourselves that we've always sought elsewhere.

Acknowledgements

First & foremost, Thank **You GOD** for your consistent favor over my life. When I thought I was at my ropes end, lost, hopeless, penniless, and in despair, **You** have always met me at the level of my needs and I am grateful for all that **You** have done and will continue to do in my life. **LORD, You** said you would make my enemies my footstool and you have done just that. Thank **You GOD** for allowing my gifts to continue to make room for me even when I don't deserve it (**ESPECIALLY when I don't deserve it**).

Magikk, thank you for loving me even when it's hard to. Your love feels like something I've seen in a movie – so unreal but amazing at the same time. Your love settles and comforts all of my fears, doubts, and insecurities. Your love makes me smile at the thought of you. Thank you for loving me without conditions and always choosing us. I pray that I reciprocate these feelings in a way that conveys love to you. I love you forever soulmate.

Mrs. Bea, you are the epitome of refuge. I am so grateful for the solace I have found within myself as a result of you being my therapist. Thank you for never giving up on me no matter how many times I gave up on myself. Thank you for always putting on your cape to save me without ever judging me and helping me grow in ways I never thought possible. I pray that you are rewarded abundantly for the decades of selfless service you have rendered to saving individuals like me.

India, thank you for always holding me down and lifting me up. More than my sister, you are my confidant, partner in crime, backbone, biggest supporter, and human diary. There is not anything I would not do for you.

Aunt Bibz, thank you for always having my back. No matter what I get myself into or how much I need you. Thank you for always showing up without a problem or complaint. Thank you for helping me remember who I am and assisting me as I found my way back to me.

Tamirra, it is to the grave with us. Friends first but sisters forever. No matter what, you have never folded on me, and I am grateful for your loyalty. Thanks for always being my voice of reason. I love you Sistah Gurl.

Dominica, thank you for believing, investing, and seeing something greater than I could in me; even when I was in my dark place. People like you are rare, and I will forever cherish our sisterhood.

Robin & Latoya, there are no words to describe the breath of fresh air you two have been in my life. Thank you both for always having my back, supporting me, encouraging me, praying for me, motivating me to be a better version of myself, and for all the memories that we have created and all the ones to come. No matter what happens, your loyalty never wavered, and I am forever grateful to have you two in my life.

Tyra, this is our season and every season after it is ours too. I remember the countless days that I wanted to give it all up, but you would not let me even amid your own struggles. Not only did you wait with me and hold my hand in that dark place, but you also cried with me, prayed with and for me, and spoke life into me. Not once did you ever complain or talk about it. You are my sister beyond the grave.

Shairra, Dontrayia, Tiffany, Lanesha, Jabreia, Patricia, Vashti, Shantel, Tiericka, Corron, Keyshawn, Kendra, Destinee, & Danielle my true friends in this life and the next – IT'S UP! Y'all ready?

To My Family, thank you for everything – the good, the bad, and the in-between. Beyond The Grave!

As I regained consciousness, I tried to become aware of my surroundings. However, I could not stop the tornado that was taking place in my head. As I connected to my senses, I could feel that I was still tied to the chair. My legs and my hands were still bound, and my eyes were still covered with a bandana. So, I knew the breeze that I felt on my face had to come from the crack beneath the door of the cellar where I was being held hostage by animals. Yes, animals. That is the only word that comes to mind to describe the husky masked men who held me against my will.

Why the fuck is my body so wet? I thought to myself. It was barely 60 degrees in the room, but my face, neck, and the top of my shirt felt like someone had thrown a bucket of water on me. I attempted to shift my body to provide my buttocks some temporary relief from sitting in the same position for so long. My attempts failed as my body seemed to be shutting down limb by limb. Instantly, I began to panic. While trying to open my eyes, I could feel that the right one was swollen shut. Fresh tears burned the back of my eyelids before leaving my eyes after realizing that my face had been beaten. More than likely, it was with the gun that was held to my back when the masked gunman snatched me. I sniffled my running snot before it could run onto my lips. Then, I felt movement.

"D, are you woke?" I heard Lilly whisper. My tears began to fall heavier. Words cannot explain how bad I felt. This was the second fucking time I had gotten my sisters into a crazy situation because of my boyfriend Dev.

"Yes, I'm up," I slurred through tears. "I don't know what that shit was that they shot in us, but it got me stuck. I cannot move anything. Are y'all okay?"

"Thank You GOD! We are good. Just try to stay still D. They shot you with some shit that is supposed to keep you sedated. I heard one say that if you try to fight it when it is wearing off, it can cause your body to paralyze. You have been all the way out of it for a couple hours. They did not sedate us though. They made us listen to them do shit to you and they recorded it to show Dev. They were trying to get him to bring the money faster for real." I had no idea how true her information was about becoming a paraplegic, but I completely relaxed my body in case it was accurate.

"Damn! How long have we been here? If they got the money, why haven't they let us go? Ain't like we know who they are." My speech was slow, and it felt as if I was straining to speak.

"Dev ain't bring the money."

"What you mean he ain't bring the money? How you know? Did they say that? They are bullshitting. He brought the money. They just being cruddy trying to get some more." I forced out angrily. My body instantly tensed up causing me to remember to relax. I had no idea why we were still here. I know he paid them the money. Shit, they only asking for $10,000. That would not even put a dent in his Dev's stash which was a few hundred dollars short of being $100,000. I would know I counted that stash every night for the last two years. Maybe they were asking him for more. I did not know what to think but damn, why couldn't they just let us go?

"When the fuck you gon' wake up and see that the nigga does not fuck with you for real?" It was the first time I heard Porsha speak since we were forced into the back of the van. I knew she was mad. Shit, I was mad too and hurt even having her in a middle of such an ugly situation. AGAIN! It had only been a little over a year since Dev's crew opened fire in the middle of our Aunt Babs' backyard at Porsha's birthday cook out because he was beefing with some of her friends from West Baltimore.

"I'm sorry this is happening, P." I lowered my head empathizing with the pain I knew my sister was feeling.

"Porsha, I know you are upset but chill out. We all done got each other in some crazy situations. This may be a little more crazy than usual but we are still in this together. No matter what. We can't chew each other's heads off or we'll never make it out of here." Lilly said sounding encouragingly.

"We're going to make it out of here, Lil. I know he ain't shit sometimes, but I know that Dev paid them. He's not going to leave us hanging y'all."

"Dev is not going to pay them D. After they sedated you, they pistol whipped you, and sent pictures to Dev. They told him to call within an hour if he wanted us to live. He did call." Lilly paused and took a deep breath.

"Of course, he did. When did he say he was going to meet them?"

"They answered on speaker and we could hear him say clear as day that they could kill us because we aren't worth ten thousand dollars that they are demanding. "

"Damn. He said that?" My heart broke and my world came crashing down around me. I know one may think that it should have broken when I first got kidnapped or even at the bullet ridded cookout or the long list of events that happened even before that, but it did not. This was routine. The more I loved him, the more dangerous it got but it was addictive, and I could not let go. Besides, I knew what I was getting into when I started messing with him.

I never knew it would be like this, but I knew what came with dealing with a hustler. My father was a hustler and my stepmother found herself in situations like this and worst throughout my entire life. Things were no different for Dev and myself. For 5 years, I had loved Dev with everything in me. I rode with him through everything. I had lost so much of my family, my friends, and myself by being with him. Though I was only 16, I knew he loved me. He just had a crazy way of showing it sometimes. Maybe it was a mere image of my distorted perception of love, but it was love to me, nonetheless. It was our love and right then, I needed that love to be more than enough for him to have my back like never before.

"Yes, D. He said that." Lilly replied softly.

"I'm scared. I don't want to die like this. I don't want any of us to die like this!

"Do y'all realize that we fuck up so much that nobody is probably even looking for us yo? They probably think we out on one of our little missions again. Being hot in the ass or something. Whatever the case, we are not going to die. We are not even going to speak that shit into existence. The niggas who took us was on some other shit. They do not want to hurt us, or they been would have. They just want the money." Porsha said reassuringly.

"Bitch, speak for y'all. My fucking face hurts like shit, so somebody fucked me up. And I still can't really feel my body." I said

"None of us can bitch! We've been tied together for hours. If we do make it out, we all fuck around and be paralyzed!" Porsha yelled.

"No, I mean like I can't even move my neck. I already feel paralyzed."

"Just try to stay calm, D" Lilly said and just as I was about to respond, a phone rang. We all got quiet and still. We were not alone. The ringing halted and a man with a very light voice began communicating on his Boost walkie talkie.

Bleep Bleep "Yo."

"We got it. Cut 'em loose."

Bleep Bleep "Bet!"

Even though the bandana was tightly secured around my eyes, it felt like I could see him getting closer. He cut the rope from our wrists and legs.

"Count to 100 then y'all free to leave." I do not know if we were all scared to count or if we were all counting in our heads but none of us said anything.

"OUT LOUD BITCHES!" he shouted causing all of us to get tense. "Y'all big mouth bitches been talking all this time now y'all want to shut up."

"1, 2, 3 . . ." we all started to count in unison.

"Nice doing business with you thickems!" he said before rubbing my cheek with the back of his hand. His touch scared me, but my body was too weak to fringe. The feel of his hand scared me more than the touch itself. It felt like snakeskin. Like one of those skin diseases. The door opened and shut. We stopped counting and were quiet for about 10 seconds before Lilly finally spoke.

"Y'all think he's gone?"

"I don't know bitch but I'm taking my chances. If I'm going to die, it's going to be trying to get the fuck home." Porsha said as she got up and took off her blindfolds. Lilly did the same. Even though my body was no longer bound, I still wasn't free. I could barely move. *Did they use dope to sedate me? Is this what a heroin high feels like?* I wondered in that moment why so many chose to use it? I had been high before. Shit, I had been high every day before then for the past year but I never felt this feeling before. Lilly took my blindfold off my face and grabbed one side of my body as Porsha grabbed the other. With all the assistance I could offer, I helped them stand me up and slowly we walked out of the cellar door into the darkness of the night.

We walked about the same speed as a turtle until we came to Greenmount Avenue and 22nd Street. I began feeling lightheaded causing me to stop in my tracks. Lilly and Porsha walked me to sit on a vacant house's step.

"Damn, they took our phones and shit. I need to use a phone so I can get Ty to come get us. Lilly, you stay with Diamond while I try to find somebody with a phone." Porsha said as she looked around for a pedestrian to use their phone. Just as she was crossing the street, an all-black heavily tinted Toyota slowed down as it rode passed and my heart started racing. My body tightened as I could feel it shutting down again. I wanted to scream but I looked around and noticed it was no one around.

Usually, even in the middle of the night you could spot a house with a light or television on not this night. Not one single house within sight showed signs of occupancy. Thankfully, the car kept going. After about 10 minutes of no activity whatsoever, a street walker strolled down the street across the other side of the street from us. Porsha ran over to her to ask her to use her phone. I closed my eyes and for the first time in a long time, I prayed as the tears begin to fall from my eyes.

GOD, I know I am the last person you want to hear from but if you please give me the strength to get up so we can make it home safe, I promise you that I will leave Devon alone for good.

Instantly, as if **HE** were sitting on **HIS** throne waiting to hear from me, my body loosened up. I swung my legs over the edge of the stoop before using all my upper body strength to sit up straight. Porsha was thanking the street walker for using her phone before returning to us.

"Stay still D. The ambulance is on the way."

"Ambulance?" Lilly and I said in unison.

"Yes, Bitches! An ambulance! Ty didn't answer the phone. Your ass needs to be seen by a doctor anyway, so that was the only ride I could think of. Besides, I'm sure Grandma would be happy to know we're at a damn hospital rather than dead in a fucking basement." It made sense to me. Shit anything made sense to me at that point. I felt like I was dying slowly. Out of all of the times I asked to die, I realized then that I really didn't want to.

"You're right!" I agreed. "I told y'all Dev was going to pay them. He may have a fucked-up way of showing it and I know things can be crazy between us, but he does love me." I said in a slight whisper. As if I had a sudden case of dementia, I forgot about what I had just promised GOD. My thoughts immediately went to Dev. I knew he was not going to leave me in no situation like that. We have been through too much together. I had sacrificed so much for him.

Ten thousand was easy to surrender after all that I had given up for him. I couldn't wait to see him and show him my face. I knew he was going to kill whoever did this shit to me. I wonder how they found us though. *We gotta move out of that house.* I been told him that. The sirens of the ambulance getting closer broke me from my thoughts just in time to catch Porsha's question,

"Are you trying to convince us or yourself?"

Chapter One

"Renee B., Tarsha H., Diamond L., let's go!" I stood up and looked at myself in the mirror. My hair was in a basic ponytail because I didn't know the first thing about doing hair and no one that I was cool with in here could do hair either. It was all good because a ponytail wasn't that bad when you could dress. Thankfully, my big sisters, Lilly and Porsha brought me packages with clothes and personals bi-weekly, so I had plenty of fly shit to wear.

"Diamond L."

"I'm coming! My bad!" I grabbed my two bags and walked to the doorway of my dorm room. I accomplished more than what I came here for. The rest of my life was up to me. I smiled as I closed the door behind me and went to look for Rachel C.

"Rachellll!" I yelled so loud that my case manager came out of her office.

"Diamond! Why are you being so damn loud?"

"My bad Ms. Sherry. I am looking for Rachel. I have some things for her."

"They're all at Pop. They went down first today. I can hold it in my office until she comes. Is that fine?" Pop meant time to eat so they were currently at the cafeteria for lunch.

"Yes ma'am. That's fine." I held up the bigger bag, "These is clothes; some new but all clean and in great condition. It's new bras, socks, & panties in there too. All of the panties and socks are new." Then I held up the smaller bag. "These are personals. It's lotions, body washes, sprays, pads, tampons, toothbrushes, toothpaste, slippers, make up, lashes. . .everything for real!"

"Wow Diamond. If I must say so myself, you have changed a lot since you first came here six months ago. I am so proud of you! Who would have thought that we would grow so close. Remember, when you first came, I was every bitch in the book. I was okay with that too!" We both giggled as she reminded me of how I was when I first came. "I told you then that I'd be however many bitches you needed me to be to make sure that you got the most out of this experience. You have a lot of new things to look forward to. There is greatness waiting on you baby girl. All it takes is for you to believe that. You must imagine your greatest self and believe in her with everything in you! Now give me a hug and get out of here and take the world by storm. And no matter what, DO NOT USE!" We hugged tightly as I thanked her, and I made my way downstairs. She was right. She was most definitely a bitch, but I respect all that she did to help me get into perspective so that I could accomplish a lot with being here. As I rode the elevator there. I thought about when I first came.

I sat in the back of the Department of Corrections' transport van trying to make sense of what was happening in my life, but I kept drawing a blank. It seemed like yesterday when me and my ex were living it up and counting it up the same, on some Bonnie and Clyde shit. That was until we were pulled over for speeding and caught a drug charge. Even though he was driving, I took the charge since his lawyer advised that I would make out better without any jail time. Without thought, I did just that not knowing that I would not get a chance to walk out the precinct on my own. My bail was initially denied. There were not enough drugs in the car to support a bail denial. I knew they really wanted Devon, my boyfriend, but they ain't have shit coming. I was not raised to be no snitch. My public defender was able to use my excellent grades in college, character reference letters from my professors, and accolades and awards from my employer to convince the judge to give me a $25,000 cash bond at arraignment. After attempting to reach out to Devon several times unsuccessfully, I finally reached out to my family. They were not pleased to just learn what was going on, but they pulled the money together came through. My grandmother refinanced her house to get the loan for my bond and my siblings put together to hire my Aunt Shelly boss, Corwin Brown, as my lawyer. He was the best criminal defense attorney in Maryland and really my only sure way to get out of this mess the cleanest. I promised to pay her the money right back but even after my release, but I could not get in touch with Devon. He had not been let completely off the hook in the case, so I just charged it to him taking necessary precautions to remain a free man even though my family wasn't buying that excuse. As the trial came to an end, I was placed in police custody at my sentencing. I was not expecting that, but I was grateful to not be going to jail. Or so I thought, I still had to spend a week at Central Bookings until my bed was ready at the facility.

"Lewis...LEWIS!" The C.O. called out to me. I snapped out of my thoughts and got off the van to go into this six-month substance abuse treatment program the judge thought would be best for me. I had always been a drinker, drinking daily, even if only wine. Lately, I'd been doing molly on top of the drinking. It increased my libido resulting in wild passionate sex for me and Devon every night. However, in the month of the trial, I had decided to stop everything, so I experienced what the judge believed to be withdrawal systems due to the drugs and alcohol leaving my system and cravings from wanting more. I knew that I was lovesick but whatever was going to get me less time, we were going to go with that. If a treatment program would keep me out of jail, I was all game. As we walked through the door, I was disgusted that I even had to stay in any facility for six months but hey, it was what it was. A fly ass middle age lady appeared from the office near the front with a blanket, sheet, and pillow which she struggled with a bit as she signed the papers for me to be released from their custody. She then turned to me.

"Hello Ms. Lewis! My name is Sherry Devon. I will be your case manager for the entirety of your stay. I am not going to make you do anything here. I won't even make you stay but if you do not comply, your ass will be going right back in that van and to prison. My hope is that you'll decide to take in the things you'll learn and store them in your mind for later even if you don't feel you need them now. You are only here for six months and it is going to fly pass before you know it! Let's make this as easy as possible." I stood there for about five seconds; looking her right in her eyes. You can always tell by how a person maintains eye contact with you when conveying information to you if they are genuine or not.

"I came here to do my six and dip. Where's my room?" I asked plain, appearing uninterestedly when in reality I was nervous.

"Six and dip. Ha! Come with me. I'll show you!" She threw her head back in laughter and spun around on her heels before walking off with me following her. She showed me where the bathroom and showers were, TV/lounge area, meeting rooms, and cafeteria were before ending at a room 111.

"Here's your room. Bed three is yours. Enjoy!" She smirked but as I looked around, I did not see a damn thing to smile about. I had two roommates. One was clearly neater than the other. I sat down on the bed next to where Sherry had placed my bedding supplies. She came back in the room, "Here are some personals; soap, wash cloth, toothpaste, toothbrush, shower slippers. You also had a package. It's being processed but it'll be up here either tonight or first thing in the morning." I nodded reluctantly. "Your stay here will only be as bad as you make it." A single tear slid down my face, but I quickly wiped it away but not fast enough. She cocked her head to the side, "Whatttt?! Not you crying Mrs. Six and Dip." Sherry sarcastically.

"Can I have some privacy so that I can get my stuff situated?"

"Yup! No problem. Enjoy your 45 minutes of privacy because your roommates will be up from dinner pop then." Right as she was about to exit the room, a man was about to knock.

"Are you Diamond Lewis? This is your package." He said.

"Cool!" I could barely carry the box it was so heavy. My sisters had everything you could imagine in the box. We could only have 10 outfits, but Porsha knew how to work the system. She made sure to buy me some leggings labeled tights and packs of t-shirts so I could wear either with my clothes to make additional outfits. Also, in the box were 3 pair of shoes, 2 pair of slippers, shower shoes, personals, a robe, magazines, and even some books. I started by putting my clothes away first. The drawers on my dresser were all intact and very clean. I was surprised considering the stories I heard about this program while I was being held at the holding facility. I lined my shoes up under the edge of my bed next. I felt like a complete bum so thank GOD for my sisters! I know how much they had to go through. It would have been a piece of cake had she been able to go to my apartment and just pack up some stuff. However, in order to get a package here, everything had to be brand new. Sitting on the bed after making it, I went through the remaining things. I sat all my personals on my dresser, then went through my books. I smiled as I fumbled through the magazines and came across a Forbes one. I'd always had a thing for numbers and finances. I was almost finished school for my bachelor's degree in accounting too. I only had three semesters left. Next, I looked through the books; 48 Laws of Power, Coldest Winter Ever, Who Moved My Cheese, and finally a Journal. Excitedly, I thought about how I could write my way through the six months with ease. I opened the cover page to the journal where I found a letter from Porsha folded between the cover and first page.

SG (Sistah Gurl),

  I cannot imagine how you feel right now but if I had to guess, I'd say irritated. LMAO. Bitch, your ass is always irritated about everything. This time rightfully so. It may seem hard right now, but trust me, if anyone I know can come out on top of this, it's you. You are a soldier; one the strongest and most loyal people I know. Which is why though it's hard for me to tell you the things I'm about to tell you but, I'm obligated to. Because you took the charges, Devon was able to get off on all the charges he was facing. Which was the plan right? Cool. However, he has not made an effort to contact any of us nor has he given us anything for you. For the first time ever, I used my spare key to check on your apartment, the day of your sentencing and nothing was out of place except for your bedroom. He had been there and packed all of his stuff, emptied the safe, and took whatever was in the other spot. The police still have your car and they will not allow me to get anything out of it. They said it was still evidence. It's all good though. If you got it once, the second time it's easier. Don't worry about anything but fulfilling your obligations to the program and coming home. We got you. Let me know if you need anything. Your friends collectively gave me $500. Lee, Lilly and I put up $300 each. Aunt Babs gave me $250. Mommy gave me $100. After getting you the contents of your package, you have $650 left. Let me know if I missed anything. Grandma said she'd have $200 on Friday but I told her no. I know you wouldn't take her money. She sent her love though and said 'Tell my baby do not worry about things that can be obtained again. She *must know that she is irreplaceable.' She's not mad at you. None of us are. How could we be? We love you and we got your back just like you've always had ours. I know how hard this has to be for you but allow us to take care for you for once. Don't worry about a mother fucking thing out here. You sit in there and get your mind together. Who knows? You may learn some something. Beyond the grave, I love you to life. Forever.*

Hold your head,

Porsha

  Against my will, the tears flowed down my cheeks as the thoughts just started rushing through my head. Mainly, how forgiving my Granny was even though I didn't deserve it. She put her house up to bail me out of jail and to repay her generosity, I banked on the nigga I put my life on the line for. Now, my grandma was stuck paying a mortgage again on a house that was paid for. Then she's doing it on her own now because her husband, Mr. Kevin, had passed away. I mean, my siblings helped here and there but they had their own households to hold down. Not only had I taken Devon's charge, but he really took all of money. Most of which belonged to me because I was the only one who saved. He liked to splurge his money, often looking like more money than he actually had, and I was the exact opposite. While wiping my tears, I promised myself two things; one, that I would get his ass back if it was the last thing I did and two, that I would pay off my grandmother's house. Interrupting my thoughts, my roommates walked in. Looking them both up and down, I examined them thoroughly. Both of them were beautiful in their own right; one was a small framed petite girl and the other was a tall big girl. The larger female was very loud as she came in.

"Welcome Dear! What is your name? I'm Rachel!" I looked at her but didn't answer. Instead, I reverted my attention to the smaller one who was sitting on her bed staring at me. "Okayyyy then! Another one of those!" she said sarcastically.

"Another one of what bitch?" I jumped up.

"Another bitch strolling in here with a funky ass attitude mad at the world like we enjoyed the high of whatever got you in this mother fucker." We stood face to face.

"This ain't what you want!" I had a lot of anger built up in me and didn't mind letting it go on her ass.

"Rachel sit your ass down!" The smaller one said as she laughed so hard that she was holding her stomach.

"Ain't a damn thing funny. I'm not gonna let anyone disrespect me!" Rachel said as she walked back to her side of the room.

"How did she disrespect you? Because she doesn't feel like talking? That's sounds crazy as you look right now!" She then started laughing again.

"Whatever!" Rachel yelled and walked out of the room. The smaller one then stood up and begin going through her drawers for night clothes. She then began undressing and replaced her regular clothes for her robe. As she was putting on her robe, I noticed a large tattoo in the middle of her back of a gorilla's head that read 'Long Live the Guerillas' over the top. She started walking out of the room but turned and said to me.

"My name is Trina. You don't have to talk now but as time goes on, you'll find that talking will make it easier for the time to go pass. The only person that can hurt you in here is you. Let me know if you need anything." Without waiting for a response, she turned and walked out. I laid there thinking about how I needed this transition to go as smooth as possible. Like my grandmother always said I had to get out of my own way. Rachel walked back in and sat on the side of her bed. I continued laying back on my bed lost in my own thoughts. After about fifteen minutes, Trina returned as well and began getting dressed. My mind thought back to her tattoo. She laid down on her bed and pulled out her book, *True to The Game*, and began reading.

"Asante Dada," I said out loud from the position I was laying in. Silence followed. After waiting a few moments for a response, I took off my shoes and jacket, grabbed my personals, robe, underclothes, and shower slippers to prepare for my shower. As I was leaving the room, Trina peeked her head up from her book.

"Hakuna Shida Dada!" I stopped and turned to face her. Our connection was sealed.

"What in the Lion King language are y'all talking about? This better not be no damn witchcraft. Trina your ass already dress like you're one of those gothic people." Rachel said in a jokingly but serious tone. We all laughed. For the first time since I got there, I felt like I might be okay. I would not let them know that just yet, but I felt it.

"No witchcraft and my name is Diamond"

"How long you have to stay?" Trina asked

"Six months. How about you?"

"One year. I got six months left though." Trina responded.

"I'm in the one-year program too. I'm only one-week in." Rachel said. "Damn!" I said in relief. Six months was looking more and more like a blessing.

"Exactly why I told you to chill! They can extend your time any time they feel like you aren't in compliance."

"True. I'm trying to be out of here on April 2, 2015! Not a single day later!" Little did I know that room would become my safe haven for six months. So many dreams, goals, stories, secrets, and tears shared in that room!

"Diamondddddd!" I snapped out of my thoughts to see my sisters, Porsha and Lilly, waving and calling me like crazy people. Damn! I knew I missed my sisters, but I never knew just how much I missed them until I saw them. They brought me a package every other week of personals and anything else I mentioned I needed when I wrote Porsha. Lilly wrote me daily; I literally have a letter for every single day that I was there from her.

"My bad. I was thinking about some shit!" I responded. "Heyyyyy bitches! Damn I missed y'all so fucking much!" We hugged for what seemed like forever!

"You look so beautiful, D." Lilly said hugging me again tightly. Lilly was older than me, but she had always been my baby. My skin was radically glowing. More importantly, I felt as beautiful on the inside as I did on the outside.

"You really do look bomb as fuck bitch. You have gained a little too much weight, but you do look good bitch. And it is definitely time to get your hair done. That ponytail is eww." Porsha laughed.

"Shut up bitch. We worked with what we had in there. Plus, my shit grew out."

"It did but let's go try Tonya's new shop because that head is a mess darling!"

"Do I have to? I kinda just want to eat and chill with everybody for real. Not into getting dolled up today." I whined and Porsha looked at me in disgust.

"Yes, it's a must and the appointments are already set. I don't know what this place done did to you but get your life together really quick bitch!" Porsha responded. We all laughed on the way to the car. Once in the car, we chatted about everything; especially catching up with who is who and what's going on in the hood. My heart broke when I thought about the fact that my grandmother moved to South Carolina while I was in the center, and I was not able to hug her or kiss her face before she left. I understood her financial situation and why she had to leave though so I respected her decision. Porsha looked over at me and asked, "What are you thinking about?"

"Grandma…" I responded as the tears begin to flow. "I feel bad like I uprooted her comfortability. I really wish things could have went differently." Lilly begin to cry as well.

"Oh, hell no bitches! We all wish things could have went differently but it didn't and there's nothing we can do about it right in this moment. We are not dealing with this shit today. No! No! No! We have cried enough over the last 14 months. Not todayyyyyyy! We are celebrating. Our little sister is home!" Porsha said looking at Lilly through the rear-view mirror sternly signaling her to shut up without saying a word.

"Bitch you are not anybody's mother. We are your sisters, not your kids." I looked back at Lilly causing her to smile. "But you are right. We're gonna celebrate for Grandma too!"

"Yesssssss! You know how she likes to drop it!" Porsha smiled. We all laughed thinking about our grandma dancing. "But bitch don't ever read me."

Chapter Two

My eyes cracked open as I heard Lilly singing while cooking breakfast. She had it smelling like Heaven in there, but I was so tired from tossing and turning all night. It was my first night in over six months staying somewhere outside of a facility. Secondly, I didn't feel right having to stay with my sister. I had never had to stay with family since I left home at fourteen, so this was an uncomfortable circumstance for me. Lilly and her husband Jerad, who was a big-time hustler from West Baltimore, must have sensed that I felt some type of way because they both consistently asking if I was okay and checking to make sure I was comfortable. Lilly and I sat up until 3am talking and reminiscing. She made sure to tell me to make myself at home at least twenty times. The thing is that most likely, I wouldn't because I wasn't going to be comfortable until I was in my own space again. Their home was small but beautiful. It was a two-bedroom, two-bathroom apartment in Pikesville, MD where I had my own room and bathroom. The entire condominium was newly developed, and Lilly had it decorated to perfection. Did I mention that Lilly was a bomb ass cook and made breakfast, lunch, and dinner daily? One would be in Heaven but not me. I still felt like I was invading their space. I could never feel comfortable in another woman's home. Securing a residence didn't have me worried though because I'd been creating a plan for the last two months. Now, I just had to work the plan. Unable to fall back to sleep, I got up and made my bed. As I made my way to the bathroom connected to my room, there was a knock at the door.

"How you know I'm woke?" I yelled at the door before Porsha busted in.

"Because I don't hear you in here snoring like a pig!" We laughed and I proceeded to the bathroom as she sat on the chair in the room to talk to me.

"What's your plans for today?"

"I'm not sure yet for real."

"Good because I'm taking you shopping and then we're going out tonight!"

"Not really in the mood for that sis."

"Not really a choice bitch! Get yourself together. Lilly made your favorites! And..." she paused.

"And what?" I asked as I looked at her seriously.

"You have a visitor." Porsha said reluctantly. My eyes lit up because I knew it was Devon. No matter what, I knew he would never just leave me high and dry. We had been through so much together. We were connected by loyalty and it was no way that he would ever leave me. In that instance, I was so happy that Porsha had made me get my hair done. I ran around the room like a chicken with its head cut off laying out my outfit and shoes. I didn't have much to choose from since I left most of my clothes I owned at the center for Rachel. I wasn't tripping though, I looked good in whatever I put on. Buttttt...maybe, if I appeared bummy, he'd be ready to drop some stacks on a shopping spree for me.

"I gotta get ready. Tell him come in and sit down. I'll be out after my shower."

"D, let's talk first."

"Porsha, I don't have time. Just do what I asked. Damn!"

I ran in the bathroom and hopped in the shower. Though, I'd showered a few hours ago before bed, I washed myself again thoroughly and groomed myself too. I knew Porsha was going to give me a long speech about how I should stop fucking with him and all of that but why? Everyone had ups and downs. I was rocking when it was sunny. Why would I leave because the storms had come? Besides, I wasn't an angel either. We had overcome a lot and we were stamped forever. Humming as I dried off, I put on my body oil and perfume before dressing in my robe. When I opened the bathroom door, I received the surprise of my life. Pete sat in the chair holding the picture of me, Trina, and Rachel that we took at an event at the center that I framed and put on the nightstand next to the bed.

"You still don't respect boundaries I see!" I screamed. He got up and placed the picture down on the nightstand before turning to look at me.

"Damn." He said looking at me up and down from head to toe. I had gained a lot of weight and though I hated it, I knew Pete loved it.

"How can I help you, Pete?" I asked uninterested in having any type of conversation with him.

"Actually, I'm here to see how I can help you." He asked and plopped down on my bed.

"Get the fuck off my bed in those jeans!" I screamed and rolled my eyes. He knew I hated that. Pete and I had a complicated past. He one of my father's workers when we met.

Summer 2000

"Diamond Lewis! You are not going to get on my damn nerves about going over that man's house. Last time you were begging me to come get you. I don't want you over there." Grandma Mae said as I plopped down on the chair. I mean she was right. My father got really drunk and went off the deep end when I was there for my school's winter break. I asked him about going home for Christmas Day so I could open my presents since his household was Muslim and they did not celebrate Christmas. One would have well thought that my ten-year-old self was asking him something extremely disrespectful since he slapped me so hard that he left a bruise of his handprint on my face. My lip even bled a little. Seems crazy, right? Well, he is this self-righteous Muslim that treats his religion like a cult. So, to address anything that opposes infuriates him and when he is under the influence of alcohol, he takes everything to the extreme. As a result, my grandmother, whom I lived with barred me from spending time with him there. He was allowed to visit me Saturday afternoons from 12pm - 3pm and he came faithfully.

"Pleaseeeee Grandma! He went to rehab so he is doing really good. He ain't been drunk not one time since he's been coming to see me." I begged. I knew he probably

was drinking after he left. I did not care. My plan was just to stay on his good side.

"Yeah right and he probably went and got drunk as soon as he left. Okay. Fine. I'm telling you now though, if he knocks your brains loose, do not – and I do mean DO NOT – call me at all." Grandma Mae said but I knew she was lying. She would have a heart attack if she knew how many times before he'd hit me and I hadn't called her. I ran up the steps to pack my backpack full of personals. I had plenty of new clothes and shoes at my father's house for the Summer. My stepmother always got my summer stuff as she shopped for her kids. I was so excited. Though I had seven siblings on my father's side, I was most excited to see my friends. See, at my fathers' house I could go outside and as far as around the corner and on the block behind his house. I ran downstairs with my backpack and could hear my grandmother on the phone with my father. I stopped at the bottom step so I could listen to her in the kitchen. "Now don't let me ever have to tell you again…Mmmhhmmm…She's ready."

Walking into the living room, I saw all of my siblings sitting around talking and laughing. I was sad to leave them. Lilly and Porsha's dad was killed in a shootout one week before Lilly was born. Lee's dad was with the feds in Cumberland doing 30 years. My mother was married to Trina and Isis' dad but he was killed when she was pregnant with Isis. When the father's disappeared so did their families. I was the only one who had a connection with my father's family. My father was not the best but it was what it was. Our mother was upstairs in Lee's bedroom sleep, but she mines well been gone too. Her routine was work all night and sleep all day. Traveling and partying on all of her days off was her favorite pastime. Our grandmother and her husband, Mr. Kevin were all we had. They took good care of us. Thank GOD for that.

"You leaving?" Lee asked peaking at my bookbag.

"Yeah." I said almost in a whisper.

"You don't have to feel bad for going with your dad. At least one of us gets to go somewhere and have fun." Lilly said comfortingly.

"Little girl, make sure you peep everything while you're over there. I want to hear about everything popping off when you get back." Porsha said. Porsha was the oldest, 14, and outside of school, had never went as far as the corner. So, she found her excitement in the stories I came home with from my father's house. They all were excited when I came back home for the summer for good. My father made sure I had fly clothes, shoes, and kept my hair done nice for school. I always made my father buy them a few things when he took me shopping for school. Did not matter if it was jacket, a pair of shoes, or just some uniforms, he made sure to look out for them in that way.

My grandmother and Mr. Kevin did the best they could to provide us with everything that we needed but those needs were not always exactly fashionable. So, I made it my business to make sure I threw them stuff in the cart as we shopped, especially Lee. He was the only boy, so I had to make sure that he was okay.

Knock! Knock! Knock! My father knocked at the door.

"Time to go. Love y'all!"

"Can I go?" Lee asked. "No but I'm going to bring you some sneakers. I promise."

"Aaaaayyyeee! Ok."

I smiled. It made me happy to make my siblings happy. We were all we had. I said my goodbyes and kisses as I closed the door behind me. My Dad only lived five blocks away, so we walked. As we got near his house, he stopped me, turned me facing him, and grabbed me by my throat. He applied enough pressure to allow me to know what he was about to say was serious but not enough to leave a clear visible bruise.

"Make this the first and last time I tell you this. Whatever goes on in my mother fucking house stays in my house or the next time, your grandmother will be burying your dumb ass. Do you understand me?" A cold chill went through my body as he let me go. I nodded my head silently in agreement. We walked the rest of the way to his house in silence.

"Hey my babyyy! I missed you so much" My stepmother, Ms. Roberta, shouted as I walked in. I forced a smile, but my mood was still damper though.

"Heyyyy!" I hugged her so tight.

"Are you okay baby?" She stepped back to look at me. I turned to looked at my father who is eyes I could feel burning a hole in my head. I swallowed hard and turned back to my stepmother.

"I am now." I replied and laid my head back on her, tightening my embrace. Before my father could get a chance to say anything, Pete walked in. Before then, I had only heard about him, but his reputation preceded him. Pete was only 15 but he was intelligent beyond his years. My father respected him, especially since he was Muslim. Most of the neighborhood hustlers respected his hustle and were impressed by his wit. He could indulge in an intellectual conversation with men twice his age and keep up, if not outsmart them. It was said that he loved to read,

and you could always catch him with a book in his hand. That time was no different. He sat in the corner on the couch waiting for my father to get himself together.

"What are you reading Pete?" I asked but didn't really care. There was just an awkward silence in the room after my stepmother went back to cooking.

"Who Moved My Cheese by Dr. Spencer Johnson." He replied without looking up from it.

"Cheese like money?"

"Cheese like dairy." He said with a sigh.

"Sounds boring."

"It would be for you. Stick to Dr. Seuss baby girl." He said as he got up and went on the front step to continue reading in peace. I determined right then & there, I could not stand his ass. He was always sarcastic. I could have cussed him out and not a person in the house would care. In fact, they would have probably laughed like they always do when I wild someone out. I did not though. Life had beat his ass enough. His mom was an addict and his Dad was doing life in New York, so he had to take care of himself. IHe did a great job at it though. I did not give a fuck about that in that moment. I still couldn't stand his ass. His struggles did not give him the right to act as if the rest of the world did something to him. We all were faced with our own struggles. I decided not to cuss him out considering I did say something to him first.

"CLOWN!" I shouted and laid back on the chair. I smiled as I thought about all the fun I was going to have for the summer.

"I can take them off. . ." He said as I finished reminiscing. He got on my nerves just as much today as he did any other day. Maybe more.

"Get the fuck out Pete!"

"Sike naw! I'm just messing with you! But seriously, do you need anything? Is there anything I can do for you?" I looked him in the eyes as he asked me, and I could sense his sincerity and I needed a lot of shit, so I wanted to oblige. However, Porsha knew I hated surprises and the fact that it was not Devon stirred some anger towards him in my soul that was greater than my love for him.

"Can you bring my son back?" We stood there staring at each other for what seemed like forever; both lost in our own thoughts. Finally, he spoke.

"I'm sorry D. I cannot bring back Lik back but, Wallahi, I wish I could daily." He said sincerely saddened. "I'll tell you what I can do. I can help you create another one." Against my will, that ice box I created around my heart started to melt, but I held my poker face.

"Get the fuck out!" I screamed before I became a victim of circumstance. He reached in his pocket and pulled out a phone and an envelope and dropped it on the bed.

"You can't make me stop loving you." He said before he kissed my forehead and walked out. I flopped down on my bed and let out a big sigh of frustration as my mind instantly went to Devon. I knew it was stupid to miss him, but I did so bad. As much as I wanted to convince myself that I just wanted to see him to get some money, the truth is that he had a spell over me.

"Diamond..." Lilly knocked as she came in with Porsha following her. "Are you okay?"

"Yup. I surely am." I answered matter-of-factly.

"You do know that it's okay to not be okay, right?" Lilly asked.

"Dr. Phillis, I said I'm okay. Don't asked me shit else about it." Sadness crossed her face and I instantly felt bad. I had to remember to treat her more delicately. "I do want to know how he knew I was here though." The room fell silent as I looked back and forth between them both.

"You know the nigga know everything." Porsha responded and I gave her a screwed-up face. "Alright! I told him but he really helped us hold you down while you were away. And I know deep in your heart, you know just like we all know that that man loves your ass to life. Get over Devon bitch. That nigga doesn't give a single fuck about you. Pete has always been the better choice. Stop blocking your blessings and fighting your feelings."

"Bitch, there is nothing to feel. I will always love Pete from a genuine place. He's my son's father but Malik is not here anymore."

"D. . ." Lilly began.

"D, what?" I shouted. "D, what? As much as people liked to think that our son's death would have brought us closer, it really tore us apart. Pete has another son on the way. Did you forget that? Let that man be happy with his little family." I said angrily.

"Okay Bitch! You know I'm gonna kept it funky with you and you're not going to cut me the fuck off." Porsha began. "Y'all were not in a relationship. He has been dating this girl for years and she loves him. However, he cannot even be the man that we both know he should be to her because he's still continuously worried about being there for you. No matter how many times you shut him out of your life. No matter how much fucked up shit you do to him. No matter how many times he has saved your ass and our asses. No matter how many times he has cleaned up the mess after Devon has fucked your life up time and time again. No matter how many fucking times you led him on. We all know that Malik's cause of death was SIDS. The medical professionals confirmed that. Yet, you still treat Pete like he murdered him just because he was in his care when he died. Where's your fucking accountability? Devon had your mind so bad that you hardly let Pete see his son. The one time you trust the most stable man in your life watch HIS son overnight, he dies. That is unfortunate and hurt all of us; INCLUDING PETE. And despite all of that, he still holds you down every time you need him and shit, even when you don't. You do not get to be mad that he impregnated the woman that helped him grieve the death of his son when he had no one else. Not even the one person that could relate the most to his pain." I stared at her with anger, but she was right.

"Bitch, fuck you!" I said as I flopped down on the bed.

"No bitch. Fuck you. That shit is wack. If you do not fuck with him, leave him be completely. Don't fuck with him when it's convenient for you."

"Bitch, you invited him here if you forgot. I did not ask about him or request to see him."

"As I should have. He paid for your lawyer and made sure your needs were met the entire time you were in that place. Yet, you were hoping it was a nigga that left you on stuck and ran off with your money after you took his charge. You are a complete mental case if you think I give a single fuck about your attitude, bitch. You're lucky I ain't tell him come get some of that cat." Porsha laughed and tried to tickle me.

"Yeah right. Whatever bitch. I wish he would have even thought about it." I responded even though it did not sound like a bad idea. I hadn't gotten fucked in almost eighteen months.

"Wait a minute. Devon stole your money?" Lilly asked.

"Bitch you know damn well you miss that dick. Say you don't?" Porsha asked before I could answer Lilly and we all bust out laughing.

"Let's go shopping." I said to avoid the question. I picked the envelope full of twenties and breath a sign of satisfaction.

"Ohhhhhh, you don't want to be bothered but his money is welcome? I got it." Porsha said sarcastically.

"It's not like that bitch."

"Could have fooled me but okay. Get dressed so we can go though."

I did feel better going shopping now that I had my own money. After I got dressed, I admired myself in the full-length mirror that laid against the wall. I looked good and I felt better. My skin was glowing, and my booty was nice and plump. I couldn't get rid of my stomach to save my life but that wasn't stopping shit over here honey. Believe me. I chuckled as threw my jacket on.

At Arundel Mills mall, we shopped for what seemed like forever before deciding to go to the food court. We all accompanied each other to our selective food stalls. Then we found a table in the cut where we sat, laughed, and talked about everything under the sun. They wanted to know what my plan was to get myself together. I didn't tell them the truth though.

"I'm just gonna go back to school. Finish getting my degree and move on from there." I started the conversation.

"Are you sure? I thought they took your financial aid because of the drug charge. How do you plan to finance it right now?" Lilly asked. "Yes, I'm sure! My plan is to grab a job doing home health care. They are charge friendly and it won't be as hard as getting a regular job. I checked online and my CNA license is active, so I mines well use it again. Plus, that'll offer flexibility for me to go to my NA meetings because they're mandatory for me to be able to complete successfully and have the charge removed. Then my financial aid will be reinstated." Lilly would go through the roof if she knew I planned on transporting drugs again and Porsha would want in. One thing I learned from this ordeal I was in; was I didn't want a co-defendant. Besides, both of them were living beautiful lives, had attained great careers, and had families to care for.

"Okay, sounds like a plan to me. You know we got your back one hundred percent." Lilly said excitedly.

"Sounds like some bullshit to me but whatever." Porsha responded. I looked up as Porsha's eyes connected with mine. "I can't put my finger on what you're up to but that whole school, home health, NA meetings bullshit sounds like a finesse to me. What are your plans for real? You are waiting on Devon to come back so you can get back on some shit?" I broke our eye connection by lowering my head, but I didn't speak.

"D, are you serious?" Lilly looked at me with pleading eyes. "You heard the judge. You're going to be doing 10 years in prison next time."

"No, I'm not! That was a scare tactic." I exhaled.

"Why don't you have any legit aspirations?" Lilly asked as she & Porsha stared at me.

"Am I being questioned by the bitches the bitches are spouses are drug dealers?"

"Bitch, that's just my baby daddy!" Porsha said as we all busted out laughing again. "Seriously though bitch.

Our hands aren't dirty. That's the difference. You just can't keep your hand out of the mix."

"Dirty hands. Dirty Money. Same thing." I said as I looked at their shopping bags. "But I rather make my own money and take mine on the chin!" I tried to reason.

"That shouldn't even be an option sis. You caught a good deal. Take that as a lesson." Lilly bargained.

"I guess. But I really don't know what to do. I'm great at a lot of things but there isn't anything that I love doing more than getting money."

"Use that skill. You are great with numbers so do something in finance. Go back to school and finish your degree. Build your own financial firm like you dreamed of since we were kids." Lilly said.

"That's why I need to make the money so I can pay for school in order to build my firm."

"Bitch, I knew your ass was lying." Porsha responded and I laughed but I looked up at their facial expressions and there wasn't any laughter there. In fact, their stank attitudes were in full flare but they were looking pass me. I turned to look behind me to see what had them in such a serious mood.

My blood pressure must have shot to its highest degree because instantly my head started pounding with a migraine. Here, I was fresh out from sacrificing my life on account of this nigga and his bitch ass had the nerve to be out shopping and enjoying his life. With a hand full of bags from stores all over the mall, he was locked in conversation with a chick who was short, thick, and wearing a dry bob. I was sure that they were bags in that mix for her as well and most definitely at his expense. Which meant they were shopping at my expense. Heated, I jumped up and made my way over to him until we were standing face to face. When I was in the center, I dreamed about the things I would say to him when I came face to face with him again. All of the disrespectful things I would do and all of the things I would expose about him. Now, I stood face to face and I couldn't utter a word. My heart wouldn't allow me to. Mentally, I calmed myself so that the tears wouldn't fall.

"Where the fuck is my money?" He was dead locked in a trance looking me over, so I punched him dead in his nose while he was off guard.

"Bitch! What the fuck?" he screamed and held his nose. The chick he was with desired to walk forward to see about him, but my face was very clear that it was not a great idea to do so.

"Bitch, do you have my money?" I punched his bitch ass again. He jumped up and drew his hand back to swing as he'd done many times before, but the difference is this time I didn't budge, nor did I flinch. Porsha flicked open her switchblade.

"Please try me bitch." She said and he know she was serious. Lilly had her thumb resting firmly on her taser ready to use it. It was a no-win situation for him.

"Bitch, I will knock your dumb ass out!" He yelled as I attempted to run his pockets. "Get the fuck off of me." He pushed me hard away from him. I put my hand up to stop my sisters from going at him.

"Just give me what's mine. I do not want to hear that 'I don't have it.' shit. If that is the case, you and Dora better use the mall map to take this shit back right the fuck now." My voice cracked as I screamed while kicking his bags. He looked up and smirked. He had me right where he wanted me; emotional. I held my hand out because my love for him was nowhere near my love for my money. There was no end I wouldn't travel to get revenge about my money.

"Here!" he shoved a stack of money in my hand.

"That's like 10 or 15. What's your number? I'll give you the rest before the end of the night."

"Naw. You do not get to have my number. Meet me down Oxygen tonight. Do not make me have to come look for you. There is no nice end game with that option." I said and turned around. I picked up my belongings and begin walking as fast as I could to Lilly's car. Making it to the car before them, I slid down the side of the car in tears. Shortly after, Lilly came out and sat next to me.

"It's okay sis!" Lilly put her arm around me to comfort me.

"It's not okay." I leaned my head on her shoulder.

"Well, it's not but it will be! You gotta believe that! I've seen you bounce back from every single obstacle life has ever thrown you! You dusted yourself off and kept it moving like only you could. You got this!" Lilly preached as Porsha strutted up finally reaching the car.

"Oh, fuck no! Get the fuck up and let's go get dolled up so we can go out and shit on niggas like him! Word is spreading that you are home now, and everybody is anxious to see you! So, fuck him. After you get the rest of your bread, dead that nigga from your mental." Porsha fussed.

"D, it's just like you used to tell us, we're going to make the best of everything we have to go through." Lilly added.

"Why do I still love him?" I whispered.

"Easy. When you really love someone, it doesn't fade away. You know that." Lilly assured me.

"Diamond. Lillianne. If y'all don't get y'all ugly asses the fuck up so help me GOD, I'm going to stomp both of y'all asses out. Now get the fuck up!" Porsha shouted.

"Y'all bitches gotta help me. Shat. I ain't been on the ground in a long time. These knees are weak baby." I hollered as we laughed.

We got in the car, blasted the music, and sang our hearts out on our way to Security Mall. There was a hot, make up artist named Star who was beating faces like bitches owed her money, so we went there to get our make up done for the night. Afterwards, I was finally in a good space. Not only was I happy to be home, I was also happy for the gift of life. I reflected on how much I had been through in my life and it amazed me that I was still alive and kicking. That was the key to life. It will not always deal a fair hand. However, if you play the hand you are dealt like it is the hand you desired; you will find that your life will be much more fulfilling. I vowed to myself that I would be more committed to living a fulfilling life than trying to change the fate of the cards I am dealt.

Chapter Three

On the car ride back to the house, I could not help but to think about Devon. We had been together since I was in middle school. We had been through a lot together. There were a lot of bad times but there were a lot of good times too. Our relationship really took a turn for the worse after I had sex with Pete. Lowering my head, I thought about my first encounter with Pete.

Devon and I had broken up and I just knew it was for good. I had decided that I wanted to wait until I was sixteen to have sex. Devon, on the other hand, had been having sex since he was twelve. He pressed up at first but once he realized I was serious about preserving my virginity, he fell back. I thought our relationship would end then, but Devon told me he was cool with my decision and that he would be abstinent until my sixteenth birthday as well. I believed him too. That was until my friend had exposed him for not only sleeping with her cousin but taking her out on dates and stuff too. I was too heart broken. He could have been honest with me and I would have understood. I knew our age difference and my grandmother's strict rules and curfew put a strain on our relationship. I was young but had fully developed breast and an ass sitting on my back. Grandma Mae wasn't playing me at all. I had all had to be on the front by

6:30pm and in the house by 7:30pm. Devon, on the other hand was seventeen and had all the freedom of a grown man. To make matters worse, I could only use the house phone and I had to sit right in the kitchen while using it so I could never call Devon and have privacy. Beyond that, my grandmother hated him. The odds were against us succeeding but I believed in our young love. I believed we were strong enough to get through anything. That was until finding out he lied and cheated on me. My heart was completely broken for the first time of many by him but no matter how bad I wanted to let go; I drove myself crazy thinking about him. The Monday after us breaking up, I was feeling really depressed about the whole situation. So, I decided not to go to school and to go to my father's house instead. I knew he would cuss me out, but he would not snitch on me.

    I ran into Pete as I walked to my father's and we walked down together. As we approached, it was several police cars out front and they were coming out of my father's house with him, my stepmother, and my oldest brother, Rhymeek, in handcuffs.

"Keep walking." Pete whispered. My stepmother looked at me with worry in her eyes as we walked pass. Just as we got pass them, my father spoke aloud.

"Strike the Sheppard and the sheep will scatter."

I knew that was a message to Pete, but he did not respond nor break his stride. I had no idea where I could go now. I thought about going to school, but I really did not want to. So, I just followed Pete quietly. We ended up at Pete's house. As he opened the door, he instructed me to take my shoes off once I entered. I was hesitant until I stepped inside. When I entered his house, it was so amazing. My stigma about addicts was all wrong. I thought they all lived in some trashy house with paraphernalia and food wrappers laying around everywhere like I had watched on TV. It was decorated immaculately with very beautiful antique furniture. Pete told me to have a seat and watch TV as he went into the kitchen. Again, I expected to watch some standard TV stations; maybe the stories or wheel of fortune but they had every cable channel you could think of, so I flicked through the TV until I found what I wanted to watch. Eventually I dozed off. Pete woke me and walked me to his room so that I could lay down. He told me to make myself comfortable and I did just that. I took off my top layer of clothes and adjusted my tights and wife beater before climbing into his bed. It was indeed the most comfortable bed I had ever slept in. I fell into a deep sleep. When I woke up, I found Pete on a palette on the floor. I shook him lightly.

"Pete." I whispered.

"What?" He asked but didn't move.

"I have to use the bathroom."

"Well, go to the bathroom. It's across the hall."

"I'm scared."

"Scared of what?"

"I don't know. Can you walk me?" He huffed but he got up and stood in the doorway as I went to the bathroom. I peed and took in the beauty of the bathroom. The house was laid to perfection. After I was finished, I washed my hands and came out to find Pete had left me and went back into the room. Just as I was about to step back into his room, Pete's mother emerged from her room.

"As-salamu alaykum."

"Heyyy...Hello...Hi..." I stuttered.

"Hello beautiful. No need to be nervous. I'm Ms. Sonya. What's your name?" She asked and you could hear her strong New York native accent.

"Diamond."

"Indeed, you are darling. Pete is very fond of you. He's never brought a lady home. Take care of my baby's heart. He doesn't let people in often."

"Oh, no. No ma'am. We're just friends. Well, he's a friend of my Dad's and my Dad was just arrested so he just brought me here just for some comfort from the situation."

"Okay. If that settles your heart." She shrugged and smiled. Her aura was very angelic. Though you she wore her hijab, it didn't take away from her beautiful face that you can tell at one time was plumper than it appeared now. You can tell Pete looked just like her. "I won't hold you up from resting doll. It's a pleasure to meet you, Diamond."

"Same here, Ms. Sonya. Beautiful home too."

"Thank the interior decorator in the room." I flashed a surprised face and she giggled. I was amazed that Pete had stylishly decorated the house given the fact that he always dressed so plainly. She went down the steps and I went back in the room. I tapped Pete with my foot.

"Get up." I whispered. "Why'd you leave me? Your mother came out her room and I ain't know what to say."

"Sounds like you did fine. Made a new friend if you ask me."

"Whatever."

"I'm sore baby girl so you gotta share that bed. I will grab a blanket and lay on top of the cover you are in. That way you won't feel violated or anything.

"Really Pete? Get your ass up here. I don't know why you were on the floor anyway. I'm not sleeping on the floor in my own room for anyone. I'll put their ass on the floor first."

"That's because you're selfish."

"I am not. You are foolish."

"You are selfish but it's not your fault. It's all you've been taught."

"Whatever. Just come on." I said holding the cover I was under open for him to join me.

"Diamond. I don't think. . ."

"Come on boy!" I said with sass. He took off his clothes except his socks, briefs, and wife beater. I looked at the clock. It was only 10:30am and I wasn't due home until 4:30pm so I planned on sleeping my day away.

"Grown ass man baby girl." He crawled in the bed next to me and soon, he dozed off. I watched him sleep and he looked so at peace; like he had no care in the world. I pulled the covers up over him and ease my arm around him.

"D. . ."

"Shhhh. I'm used to cuddling with my teddy bear so this is the only way I can fall asleep."

"I was going to ask can I hold you." He lifted his head and looked me in the eyes.

"Yes." I turned and faced the wall anticipating feeling his arms around me. This was the very first time I cuddled with anyone outside of my baby cousin. Against everything I thought I would feel when I had this experience, grown, sexy, horny even; surprisingly, I felt safe. I dozed off for a few hours and panicked when I did not feel Pete next to me. Just as I sat up, he walked in the door with food for us both and my favorite beverage, Pineapple soda and a bottled water for himself of course.

"I see you finally got up." He laughed.

"Why'd you leave me? I was nervous when I woke up and you weren't here."

"I had to handle something, but I thought about you. You do have to eat right?"

"Doesn't matter. You should have wakened me up. I would have walked you."

"That wouldn't have been a good idea."

"Why not?"

"Because it's still school hours."

I looked at the clock and it was only 1:15pm. It seemed like time was going so slow. I also noticed that the food we were eating came from Torino's. I knew firsthand that my father and his crew where beefing with the guys that hustled up there. I put two and two together, but I didn't say anything though. We ate and talked a bit. Pete was cooler than I thought and smarter than I wanted to believe too. Eating only made me more tired. After using the bathroom, I crawled back into the bed. Pete did the same.

"Don't leave me this time." I said. More concerned with him getting locked up than me actually being alone.

"You got that." He held me as I faced him and buried my face in his chest. His oil smelled so amazing on him. His breathing got heavier, so I figured he was sleep. I lifted myself and kissed him dead on the lips and to my surprise he kissed me back. We kissed for what felt like forever. The more we kissed, the more our clothes came off. As he climbed on top of me, we were both completely naked and everything I desired about my sweet sixteen went out of the window. I stopped him as he reached his designated position between my legs.

"Wait!" I said and he hopped up.

"I'm sorry. You do not have to do this at all. Damn. I'm tripping. I'm sorry D." He said nervously.

"Peteeee!" I said out loud. "Calm down. I was just gonna say I'm a virgin so you may want to get a towel. Please take your time and be gentle with me."

"Damn. For real, D. Wow! Are you sure you want to do this? Do not feel pressured at all. I will not look at you any different if you do not want to do it. Dead ass."

"Pete." I sighed. "Just get the towel please." I crawled out of bed as he went to his closet and grabbed three towels. He laid them out on the bed, and I laid on top of them. I experienced my first three orgasms. My life as well as my relationship with Devon changed that day. Not only did I allow Pete to take my virginity, but I got pregnant. Devon and I never recovered from that. It did not matter how many times he had cheated on me or how many bitches I had to fight with or deal with coming to me about him before then. I should have known then that things would have never been the same.

Maybe convincing me to take the charge to get him off was his plan of get back. It was my decision to agree though. Had my decision only affected me, I would have been okay with that, but I do not know if I could ever forgive myself for hurting my grandmother. That woman was my heart. She was the only person on this Earth that I knew loved me with absolutely no conditions. She was my rider and had been since the day I was born. Tears welled in my eyes as I thought about her, but I fought them back. I missed her so much. I had not seen her since my sentencing court date. I made a mental note to visit her as soon as I could so I could take her out to dinner, shopping, and leave her a few dollars. I owed her a lot more than that, but I smiled at the thought of possibly making her smile. Then I dozed off for the rest of the ride.

Chapter Four

Astonished is the only feeling I could put my finger on as I walked into the night club where my coming home party was being hosted. Though the venue had many celebrations happening that night, the family had done a great job at making sure people knew I was amongst the celebrated. Putting on my best catwalk, I sashayed my way to my section like I owned the club. Everyone was there; including every one of my siblings; even my baby sister, Isis, though she was only 20 at the time. I have no idea how they pulled that off, but it did not matter. I was happy to have all my loved ones in one place. Feeling a tap on my shoulder, I turned around to a surprise.

"Hey Babyyy!" My mother hollered over the music as she reached out for a hug. I hugged her back. I stepped back and admired how beautiful she was and by the look of her attire and jewelry, how well she was doing. Painfully, I had to also think about how well she was always doing without me or any of us for that matter. She always had funny timing. You never knew when she was in town or when she would even show her face. My mind drifted to the different times I really needed her, the disappointment of her absence, and the risks I took in order to care for my siblings in her absence. It hurts me to know how I craved her presence and she let me down every time.

"Wassup Ma?" I asked flatly as a result of my overthinking. Then, I turned my attention to the club's crowd. The club got packed quickly. I scanned the different sections. Everyone was having a great time and partying without nonsense. That made me smile.

"I've missed you baby. I think about you all the. . ."

"Not tonight." I cut her short. Looking her right in the eyes, I repeated, "Not tonight!"

Then, I walked off making my way to the bar. There were plenty of bottles in my section. The fact was that, until this moment, I hadn't even thought about drinking. Staying sober was a part of my probation since I had to report to drug court but I was feeling like I needed a few drinks. I put my face in my hands for a second before running my fingers through my weave as I shook my head.

"Can I buy you a drink sexy?" A familiar voice asked as I turned around to Devon grinning. I shifted my entire body to face him.

"Where's my money?" I'm sure he could sense the seriousness that my voice, stance, and facial expression conveyed.

"Calm down Tyson. It's right here." He held up a Zales gift bag and extended to me. As I snatched the bag and looked inside. On top of my $40,000 sat three boxes. I was so excited because I absolutely loved jewelry, but I did not let it show. Acting unimpressed, I smiled slightly without looking inside the boxes and attempted to walk away.

"You didn't answer my question. Can I buy you a drink?"

"I don't drink anymore."

"Ohhhh. Rightttt. Drug treatment!" He said before breaking out into a fit of laughter. I just stood there, almost stuck. Anger filled my veins as I battled the tears that fought to be free. I did not find a single thing funny about all that I had sacrificed to have his back. Yet he was right here, laughing in my face at the reality of it. I held my wide eyes open knowing if I blinked, the tears would flow, and I would have definitely felt defeated. I was not in position to let him win anything else in my life.

"Are you okay beautiful?" Pete slid up so close behind me that I could feel his breath on my neck. Saved by the bell. I turned around to face Pete.

"Yes baby. I'm fine." I turned back to face Devon. "Thanks for the gifts. See you around." Similar to how I walked into the club, I sashayed back to my section with Pete holding my hand for stability.

"You gotta stop walking like that. You're making different parts of my body happy." I looked back and peeped down at Pete's semi-hard bulge. He was dressed in all black Armani from head to toe. I was surprise, not at attire as he always dressed dapper for special events. More so that he was in a club and outside of his Muslim attire as he was serious about his religion. He looked very nice though. I thought back to how when we were younger, he used to be on the block reading books about his religion. I also smiled as I thought about the fact that he was the only man in my life that never changed on me no matter what. As we approached my section, I was greeted by some more family and friends. We danced a bit and laughed more than that.

Soon the DJ started playing love jams, so I went to find a seat. I didn't want shit else to do with love. Love had me out here looking crazy and feeling even crazier on the inside. Falling in love again was not an option for me. I just wanted to enjoy the rest of my life in peace, chasing paper. Looking around for a seat, I chose to sit next to Pete on a loveseat lounger and lay my head on his shoulder. He smelled so good like always. I could just lay on him and smell him forever. He rubbed my back as he sang along with the lyrics to Wale's 'Lotus Flower Bomb.' I'm not sure if it was his scent or the fact that I hadn't had sex in along while, but his touch had me hot and bothered. The thought of sexing Pete wasn't a bad idea considering that the sex was always amazing. The issue was that he got so attached afterwards. If only there was a world where we could have sex and be good friends without the mushy stuff, I live in it for the rest of my days. My thoughts were interrupted by Porsha tugging my arm.

"Let's go bitch. Y'all can do all this boo loving shit later on darling. It's time to fuck this dance floor up right now though." I kissed Pete on the cheek and promised to be right back. He smacked my ass as I got up and I looked back and gave him the eye. My joy was so authentic in that moment. My family, friends, and I danced like there was no tomorrow. Taking a break from dancing, I looked around the club at everyone enjoying themselves. I watched my sisters leave the DJ booth as my favorite song, 'Love in This Club' started to play. Lilly looked up and winked at me as I started moving my hips to the music. My brothers were ordering more bottles. My family was dancing, talking, sipping, and having a great time. I should have been focusing on the present moment; I'd overcome the hard part and I had a couple dollars to get back on my feet. However, no matter how much I told myself that, my heart was still aching. My mind kept drawing back to Devon's laughter and I thought about all the losses I experienced as a result of loving him. I lifted my head and my eyes landed right on Devon having a great time with the occupants of his section. He looked up at me for a few seconds before reengaging in the fun with his friends.

"Can I have this dance?" Pete asked as he slid up and put his hands on my waist.

"Surely can!" I leaned my head back on him as he moved closer. In sync, we danced and soon, we were lost in our own world. Smiling ear to ear, the more I danced on Pete as he leaned against the wall, the more I could feel my pussy throbbing.

Opening my eyes, I immediately saw Devon glaring at me, so I decided to show off. I positioned Pete on the lounge chair and straddled his lap as Wale's 'Bad' starting to play through the speakers. I danced on him as if I was riding him and soon Pete's manhood was at full attention signaling that it was time to go. He pulled me closer to him.

"Was all of this just a show or am I going to be able to feel that warm pussy tonight?"

"I'm waiting on you." I licked my lips and kissed him on the lips.

"Let's go," Pete said as he nodded his head toward the door. Just like that, I made my rounds saying my goodnights and we made our way to his truck. Being the gentleman that he is, he opened my door and closed it behind me before making his way to the driver's side. Once he was in, he reached in the back of the car and brought his hand forward with two dozen of daisies.

"Ohhhh! So, you just knew you were taking me home? Or you were intending to give your bitch my favorite flowers?" I asked but before he spoke, he let out a sigh of irritation.

"I attempted to bring them to you in the club, but they wouldn't let me in with them, so I just laid them on the backseat. Furthermore, I do not have a bitch. My son's mother, as you are going to address her, and I decided to take a break. Had we not, you would have been left in the club with a wet ass and I would have been on my way home to give her this stiff dick. You of all people know I am not them niggas you are used to fucking with. Let us not kill the vibe of the night." He was right. Pete was everything that a woman could ever ask for; he was a provider, protector, spiritual, faithful, and loyal to a fault. If only we could have rewritten our history, we could have had a bright future.

"Whatever!" I said as I rolled my eyes knowing damn well that he'd just put me in my place. I smelled my flowers and inhaled Daisy by Marc Jacobs. "Hell No! Are you serious?" I was excited like a kid in a candy store.

"Your bag is in the back seat. You knew I was going to get you right." He smirked. Did I forget to mention that he was romantic and thoughtful? Pete was the total package. I laid my flowers in the back seat and slid my shoes off. I positioned myself to face him as I unzipped his pants. He assisted me by laying his chair back just a little more. His dick was already at full attention as I pulled it through his briefs hole. At a red light, I kissed him passionately as I massaged his dick. I leaned back from our kiss and licked my lips while looking him in his eyes. As I took his dick into my mouth, I moaned in pleasure as I inhaled. He dicked smelled like he'd just hopped out the shower right then and there. That was one of the main reasons I loved giving him head. Gently, he pushed his dick further into my mouth before pulling it out and gently forcing it a little further in the next thrust. I opened my mouth wider to welcome his large dick as he pulled it in and out of my throat. Up and down, up and down I sucked as he moaned in ecstasy. Feeling his dick start throbbing, I knew it was almost time, so I sucked faster and deeper until I swallowed every bit of his explosion.

"Damn!" He exhaled as he pulled in front of his place. "Go get ready for me." He said as he tossed me his apartment's keys. I gathered my gift bags and flowers as I slid on my shoes. I hopped out of his truck and let myself into his house. I turned the light on as I shut the door behind me. Pete had left a trail of rose petals that led to the bathtub. I turned the water on to run a bath before my attention went to a three-tier shelf sitting in the bathroom. Sitting on the bottom shelf were a pair of slippers and a robe. On the second shelf was a hand towel and a bath towel. On the top shelf were two washcloths, Dove exfoliating bodywash, a toothbrush, toothpaste, mouthwash, and Dove deodorant. I picked up all the personals and set them on the sink before running my bath water. I brushed my teeth and thoroughly washed the makeup off my face then undressed and slid into the hot bath I had prepared. Closing my eyes and sliding down into the bath, I relaxed.

"Feels good?" Pete asked.

"Mmmm. Yesssss." I responded but did not open my eyes. I was not surprised that I didn't hear him come in as he was always light on his feet. He tapped my foot and I lifted so that he could massage it. He did the same for my other foot and my legs. Afterwards, he washed my entire body from head toe. I stood as he wrapped me in the bath towel.

"I'll give you a minute." He said as he undressed and hopped in the shower attached to his tub. Before joining him in the shower, I utilized that time to wrap my hair up with a silk scarf and clean up the trash from the packages. Afterwards, I dressed in the robe and slippers and went into his bedroom. I laid on my stomach and dozed off as soon as I got comfortable. Soon, I woke up to Pete's strong hands were rubbing the back of my thighs under my robe. Instantly, my pussy got wet. I spread my legs a little to give him access to where I wanted his hands. He massaged my legs more; moving further and further upward before spreading my legs wide apart. Excited for his touch I could feel the wetness of my pussy without my hands anywhere near it. Moving up, he caressed my ass firm but gently. Just as I felt his tongue on my clit, I let out a small moan. He tapped me signaling me to turn on my back and I obeyed. I spread my legs wide open causing my robe to open and he kissed on the insides of my thighs, slowly making his way up to my pussy. Obviously starving, he ate until I came three times. He worked him way up to my nipples which he latched onto the right one like a baby while rubbing the other one. Feeling the need to take control, I asked him to lay down as I got up and removed my robe completely. I grinned as I crawled up between his legs and took him into my mouth. Up and down, I sucked consistently until exploded in my mouth. I continued to suck. Once his dick was hard again, I climbed on top, balancing my body on my feet as I rode him until he reached his second blast of ecstasy. Exhausted, I rolled off of him unto my stomach beside him. However, he was ready for round three, so I arched my back as he positioned himself behind me. Without warning, he thrust his dick into me before pulling it out and repeating. Always knowing how to please me, I deepened my arch so he can dig deeper. I could almost feel him smirking as he plunged me over and over again. My body felt amazing while he held my hips and brought me to pleasure repeatedly before cumming himself. Both of us were drenched in sweat as we collapsed together. Both of us laughed as he rolled over next to me. We just lay there as we relax to catch our breath. After a few minutes, we opted to shower together again. After drying off, I laid down as Pete went into another room to make a call. Just as I was dozing off, I felt him slide in bed and put his arms around me.

"You're getting that tattoo covered." He whispered in my ear in reference to the big tattoo I had on my back that read 'Devon' with hearts, and lock & key. Devon was my first love. I got that tattoo right after I had Malik. I never had considered getting it covered but that wasn't an argument I was willing to have and ruin this wonderful night.

"Yeah, I know." I replied as he pulled me closer to me. The one feeling I always looked forward to when we cuddled still resonated, safety. I closed my eyes and slept better than I had in a long time.

Chapter Five

Though, I had urges here and there to drink, I was not convinced that I was an addict. That did not stop me from fulfilling my obligation to drug court though. I attended five meetings a week in order to stay in compliance. The meetings were so cool though. You were liable to hear and see anything. Truly, it was never a dull moment. I could choose any five meetings I wanted every week so, I opted to go to one Monday-Friday to give myself some balance. Trina had passes to come out to Narcotics Anonymous events, so my Saturdays sometimes consisted of a day full of NA meetings followed by a NA dance. They were always lit. I never knew that people could have so much fun sober; mainly myself but I thoroughly enjoyed it. Eventually, I snagged a job at the center where I went for my NA meetings as a Front Desk Associate.

In addition to the good things I had going on, for my birthday in July, Devon had copped me a car. We still weren't on the best terms. In fact, I had gotten good at avoiding him unless he had something for me. Pete helped me get an apartment in Columbia, and though it was an efficiency, it was very spacious. I was content with life which consisted of home, work, meetings, sex with Pete every night, and dates with Devon every now and then. I wasn't even spending time with my family like I used to. As well as I thought I had things figured out, chaos and confusion were written all over my situation. I figured if I kept it real with them both, then everything was fine. Well, not all the way real. Pete knew that I was dating someone, but he didn't know that it was Devon. Devon knew I had a friend, but he didn't know it was Pete. I know it's messy, but at the end of the day, I was single and that is how I was living life.

    My hair was growing. My skin was glowing. I was happy for once in my life. Well, almost. I tried to convince myself that I was just fucking with Devon for what he could give me. I know. I lied to myself knowing that I really wished things were different. I appreciate the couple dollars that came along with dealing with him, but the reality of the matter is that I did not need it. Pete took good care of me financially and covered all my needs. The only thing I paid on my own was my electric bill and car insurance. He had been very supportive throughout my ordeal and especially since I had been home. On some occasions, when he had time in his schedule, he even went to my meetings with me. But it was a Friday and that meant date day for Devon and me. I never worried about running into Pete because his routine for Fridays was like clockwork. He devoted his Fridays to Jumu'ah, feeding the homeless, and teaching his class for newly converted Muslims or those seeking to learn more about Islam.

Bopping my head to the music, I cruised down I-83 making my way to Angie's Seafood. After circling the block three times, I finally found parking. I looked around as I could have sworn it felt someone watching me. I shrugged it off as paranoia and went inside. I joined Devon at our favorite table.

"What's up sexy?" Devon got up to pull out my chair.

"Everything. What's up with you?" I replied as I took a seat.

"Way too much shit to cover dinner!"

"Oh, really? Spill the beans nigga." I giggled.

"Two workers got knocked off. One had a gun; fully loaded. We're beefing with some weak ass niggas from Monument Street and I'm losing too many good men. Then to top it off, I got a baby on the way." I thought I was going to faint right where I was because for the life of me, I could not breathe. Quickly, I grabbed control of myself.

"Wow! Congratulations! You're going to be a great Dad." Before he could respond, our normal waitress Jazmine came to take our orders.

"Hey y'all! What y'all getting? The usual?" "Yeah, that's good for me." He responded.

"Naw, just a double shot of E & J for me." I looked up at her. "Matter of fact, three double shots."

"You're not supposed to be drinking D!"

"Shid! We're celebrating! You are about to experience one of the best feeling in your entire life."

"Yeah but that has nothing to do with you and your sobriety!"

"Nigga please! Now you're worried about my sobriety. You were just in the club trying to buy me a drink a few months ago. Don't worry about me just like you ain't worry about my ass them fourteen months I was fighting for my freedom thanks to you." I let out a wicked laugh. It was the only way I could convey the hurt I felt on the inside. Jasmine drought the drinks back and I threw back two double shots and slid him one. I requested three more double shots.

"Diamond, you were my co-defendant. I couldn't fuck with you. I had to stay away from you. My lawyer advised me to do that."

"Righttttttt! The same lawyer that told you to convince me to take your charge, right? You want to know what's crazy?" I asked, but continued before he could answer. "You did not bother to get me a lawyer and you had my money. Did your lawyer also advise you to steal my fucking money, splurge it on your bitches, and never send me a single fucking dollar? Fourteen months. Fourteen months nigga. I lost everything because of you. I was three semesters from finishing my degree. Now I cannot even get financial aid because I have a fucking drug charge. You don't give a fuck though. You were not expecting me to survive that shit. You expected me to turn on you. Which is completely crazy bitch because I am the most solid mother fucker you have ever had in your life. But I am a fucking joke to you, right?" I asked just as Jazmine returned with the second round of drinks. I slid one over to him. "Drink up!"

"Diamond! Stop!" He said sternly.

"Stop what? Celebrating? Absolutely not. My nigga, you've been waiting a long time for this. Who's the lucky lady?" He looked at me and threw the double shot back. He didn't answer my question. He just looked at me. I threw back my two double shots. "Cat got your tongue?"

"D. That's it! No more drinks yo."

"You always did think you were my father, didn't you? Well, you're not. Now you got your own kid to boss the fuck around. To think, all these years I thought your nuts didn't work. When reality has been clear as day since the first day, I met you; it's us that doesn't work. Everything we collaborate on is so toxic making it impossible to produce anything healthy."

"D, you're hurt and you're saying anything. I still love you and am willing to make it work. We can bounce back. Always could and always have but you keep fighting it. We can still be the family we have always wanted to be."

"First thing first. We never were and never will be family nigga. I am not playing Mommy to another bitch kid! Ever! No, thank you. Secondly, fighting it? Ha! Let us not get started about fighting. I was fighting when I was sitting in that holding cell with a bitch that was ill, repeatedly throwing up and shitting on herself while I called you over and over with no response and no bail. I was fighting when I finally got a bail and learned that you had left our apartment with all of my money. I was fighting when I was cried myself to sleep night after night in a treatment center, heartbroken because you had not sent a package, a letter, or even a word through someone. Nothing. Absolutely nothing. That's what I got from the one person that I lost everything for. I was fighting when I thought that you were out here holding it down, preparing for me to come home. But you were not. When I realized you were a bitch, I threw those gloves in. There is no fight left in me for you Devon. Refusing to be with you is a choice I'm choosing willingly." I said and surprised myself. I was drunk and my broken heart was talking at this point. I'm not sure if it was because my system was fresh or because my pressure has flown through the roof, but I was starting not to feel good. More than likely, I had drunk to fast.

"Meka."

"What?" I asked confused.

"Meka." He repeated.

"What Meka?"

"You know what Meka. We only know one Meka."

"What about her?"

"That's my child's mother."

"Shymeka?"

"Shymeka." He nodded. Time froze. Meka was family. We grew up next door to each other. Closer than a friend but not as close as my sister, she was like a cousin to me. Her mother helped my grandmother nurse my mental back to a healthy space when my son died. I could not believe she would fuck my nigga. She broke the code. I could not control the tears. I did not try to hide them either. I was hurt. I was disappointed in Meka. I was disappointed in Devon. Most of all, I was disappointed in myself. Repeatedly, I let this man into my life to hurt me time and time again. I was in love with my enemy. I got up to leave.

"Diamond, please sit down!" Against my better judgement, I obliged. "Diamond, you know I love you to death and there is nothing I wouldn't do to protect you, including your heart. You know that. This will not affect us at all. I can promise you that! She knows her place and will not cause you no drama at all. I felt I'd be less of a man if I didn't tell you." I lowered my head as hot tears found their way down my cheeks. My homegirl had already told me about some pregnant chick at Karaoke night bragging about how the baby was his and how he promised to take care of her. I did not want to believe it. I needed it not to be true. Now it really hurt to know it was my childhood friend. I don't know what hurt more, the fact that I secretly continued to have hope for us knowing he'd never change or the fact that I fooled myself into crawling into his web again knowing that I wasn't strong enough to walk away until it hurt too bad to stay. I used the dinner napkin to dry the tears from my face and looked him in his eyes.

"The only thing I know is that no matter how good I was to you. . .no matter how much I hold you down. . .you never loved me the same. You are unable to take care of my heart because you never valued it. Every chance you get to make me look like a clown, you do. I'm done with the circus. Enjoy your life with your new family." I stood up to leave and he grabbed my arm.

"Don't do this to us D. Please don't give up on me. I can fix this. Come on. Just give me a chance!"

"Give you a chance? GIVE YOU A FUCKING CHANCE? The fucking nerve of you – you bitch ass nigga. All I have ever given you was chances – chance after chance after chance...AFTER CHANCE! You know what that got me? Heartbroken, broke, broken, and alone. Not only do you repeatedly do shit to cause disruption in my life, you also leave me to clean up the mess. So, tell me what am I giving you a chance to do? Bring more pain to my life? More failure? Continuous stupidity? Too late. You have already ruined my life bitch and I hate you for that. Over and over again, you have made me me look like a complete fucking idiot. Got bitches laughing at me because you are out here doing dumb shit. Like getting a bitch pregnant that grew up with me like family. It is unfixable mother fucker! I gave you plenty of chances to *fix it*. Over fifteen fucking years' worth of chances! Over fifteen fucking years of my life I dedicated to being great to you while all you did was shatter my fucking heart every time the opportunity presented itself. I wish you death mother fucker." I snatched my arm away from him and scurried past the patrons who were now looking as I made my way to the door. With apologetic eyes, I looked at the restaurant's owner who was a friend of my mother's, and she nodded her head in understanding.

    I did not even bother to get my car. Staggering, I walked around the corner to my Aunt Babs house in Perkins Projects. I decided to check on her while I was in the area and I could also catch a few hours of rest to sleep the liquor off. I obviously could not handle it anymore. As I approached her house, I saw my brother Lee and little cousin Rell sitting on the front.

"Damn Hollywood. Where have you been bitch?" Lee asked and all three of us busted out laughing.

"Fucking my life up some more! Where's my aunt?" I shouted louder than I intended and instantly, I felt woozy and unstable. I stumbled as I attempted to walk up the two steps that lead to her front door.

"Whoa! Sis, you good?" Lee caught me from falling. Something was wrong, I couldn't put my finger on it, but I felt like shit. I had 4 double shots of E&J. That was nothing compared to what I was used to drinking. However, that was before I had eleven months of complete sobriety. Before then, the longest I went without using a substance was a day or two, if that. Lee helped me sit on the step. Aunt Babs came walking around the corner. I looked up and attempted to speak and nothing came out but vomit and streaks of blood.

"Call an ambulance." Aunt Babs shouted out loud to anyone. "It's okay baby! We are going to get you to the hospital. Where's your car?" I could hear her clearly, but I could not reply. I was gagging for air as I spit up every single thing that I had eaten for the past few days. The ambulance arrived shortly and took me to Johns Hopkins. I was rushed in the back where they began running all types of tests. The doctors did a great job at whatever it was that they needed to do because soon, outside of being drowsy, my body felt numb.

"Bitch, get up!" Feeling a light push, I struggled to open my eyes as the light was too painful to bear. I felt hungover but I knew that could not be true because I never got hungover. Up until now, I could not tell you anything about the experience. Slightly, I opened one eye and saw Porsha.

"Hey...bitch! I have... so much...to tell you!" I struggled to say. My mouth was so dry. I tried again to open my eyes. "Turn...the...lights...off." After Porsha turned the lights off, I slowly opened my eyes.

"What the fuck is up with you yo? You're on some dumb ass goofy shit. You were doing do good! You only had one month until your one-year celebration! What happened D?"

"Water..." I whispered. Porsha stepped out of the room and came back with a cup of ice. I ate a few pieces of ice then let some sit in my mouth. After the ice melted and my mouth felt a bit more lubricated, a single tear came down my face.

"What?" Porsha asked with her eyebrow raised.

"Devon told me he has a baby on the way."

"So, the fuck what! When the fuck are you going to let go? Fuck him. FUCK HIM!" Porsha said unphased.

"By Meka."

"What Meka?" I finally captured her attention.

"Shymeka. Next door to Grandma. Ms. Ann's daughter." Porsha's mouth dropped once I dropped that bomb.

"Are you fucking serious? How fucking low can a mother fucker go? Damn, I'm sorry sis!" She came and started rubbing my hair and suddenly I noticed that my wig was off.

"Where the hell is my goddamn wig?" Porsha bust out laughing. "Girl, I took it off you last night.

You were sweating and I didn't want you to mess up the texture of it." "Last night? That explains why I feel like I'm starving. What you bring me to eat?"

"Nothing at all. I'm boutta go to work. Pete went to get you something I think."

"Pete! What is he doing here? He cannot be here!"

"Too late bitch. He's been here since like two hours after you got here." Before I could respond Pete knocked as he came in. Porsha & I looked at each other. She knew this conversation wasn't over. "Well, I gotta go!"

"Have a great shift sis! Do some actual work tonight." Pete said as he and Porsha hugged.

"I will not. They only pay me enough to show up." We laughed and Porsha kissed my cheek before leaving. Pete stood there looking at me blankly. I hated when he did that because I couldn't sense his emotions.

"I already know." I said as I closed my eyes. "You can't be more upset with me that I am with myself."

"I'm not upset. I'm disappointed. You were doing so well. Everything was in place so *who* made you do this?"

"Me. Every decision I make begins and ends with me."

"Diamond Mae Lewis, I'm only going to ask you one more time. Who made you do this?" Pete asked me firmly.

"Pete, I answered you! Besides, who's to say it had to be a who. Why does it have to be someone? Damn!" I looked in his eyes and they saddened.

"Say less." He shrugged and smirked as he set down in the visitor chair. On several occasions, I attempted to make small talk with him, but he gave me short answers. His only communication was with the medical staff who were tending to me and handling business with his employees. I knew that it was all going to fall apart but the chaos of it all fed my adrenaline like a natural high. But like all highs, the crash had to happen sooner or later. These were real people lives that were at stake. People who didn't deserve to be in the midst of unnecessary foolishness, especially Pete. I looked over at him as he sat reading The Sunnah and its Role in Islamic Legislation by Dr. Mustafa as-Siba'ee. That's one of the things I loved about him. He was not perfect by a long shot, but he was true to who he was. Pete lived a simple, but meaningful life. He hustled when he was younger, but he promised himself that once he turned twenty-five, he was done with that life and he kept his promise. He went to school to get his CDLs straight from high school and bought himself his first truck for his 21st birthday. He had no parents literally. His father was never coming home for some murders he had committed in a gang war. Ms. Sonya died six months before I had Malik and then we lost Malik the following year. None of that stopped him from achieving his goals. If anything, he spent more time at the Masjid or in his books. Most teenage hustlers would quit school but not Pete, he had a vision and he chased it. I used to laugh at the many times, I saw him on the block hustling, studying, and reading his schoolbooks. Yet, against all odds, here he was 29 and the owner of his own trucking company. If only I had his perseverance. I smiled as he glanced up at me. Catching my gaze, he maintained eye contact with me.

"I'm sorry Pete."

"Don't be sorry. Be careful." He stared me in my eyes, and I felt bad. He had my best interest at heart; always had. Just as I lowered my head, the doctor knocked while coming in.

"Hello Ms. Lewis. Do you remember me?" I nodded my head confirming. "How are you feeling?"

"Much better Doc, honestly."

"Good, I have your results back from the tests we ran, and I'd like to share them with you as well as discuss follow up care. Are you up to that? And if so, would you like your friend to step out?" I looked at Pete and he nodded that it was shrugged indicating it was up to me.

"Yes, I'm up to it and he can stay. He's family."

"So, your blood work, urine, and cultures all came back normal. Good news, you were not experiencing alcohol poisoning."

"Okay. That is a good thing. Maybe it was because I have been sober for eleven months before I drank last night, and I over did it a bit."

"That contributed to how you were feeling but you're also pregnant." We tested your urine, your blood, and your ultrasound as we were testing for alcohol poisoning." I paused as I let the words marinate in my mind. Pete was now up, holding my hand. Speechless, I didn't respond so he continued. "I've put in an order for you to get a pelvic ultrasound to assure that the baby's health was not affected by the alcohol consumption. A transporter should be here to get you shortly. Do you have any questions or need me to explain anything further?"

"Do you know how far along I am?"

"Hold on one second." He stepped out to the nurses' station and came right back in with ultrasound pictures. "She is about 17 weeks."

"She?" Pete asked.

"Yes sir! It's a girl." The doctor replied. I was still processing what was going on. Tears started flowing down my face freely. "Oh no! What is wrong?"

"You're going to be okay D. Do not overthink everything and stress yourself. I got you. You know that." Pete said and kissed my forehead. Fear crept over me as Malik crossed my mind. I had never considered having another child. Not because I did not want to be a mother, but because my fear of losing another child was greater than my desire to have another one.

"I know. I am not sad. These are tears of joy." I said and smiled. *Who am I to question GOD?*

Chapter Six

Christmas carols were blasting as I wobbled around the kitchen fixing Breakfast. I was more than ready to have the baby but this little girl was stubborn. Thank GOD that though we started off rocky due to my lack of knowing she even existed, my baby girl was growing perfectly fine without a single issue. My doctor informed me that she would have to go through some tests at birth to see if there are any birth defects that couldn't be tested while she's in the womb. That was fine because no matter how she came out, I was going to be the best Mother to her. Above everything, I would protect her to the best of my ability and make sure that nothing or no one would ever hurt her. I thought back to when I needed protection and my own mother was not there to help me.

Noooo!" My seven-year-old-self whined.

"Shhhh!" The monster whispered. *"Just go to sleep princess. This is a dream"*

"I don't want to. Please leave. Just get out of my grandmother's house."

"Oh you want me to leave? Just get out of your grandmother's house, huh?" He asked before slapping me. "Shut the fuck up right now or all of you mother fuckers will be homeless because who's going to pay the bills when I leave?" He said quietly through clenched teeth. I could smell the alcohol seeping through his pores. I didn't respond. "Exactly. So just lay back. It's going to feel good." Tears streamed from my eyes as Grandpop eased his hand in my panties and rubbed my clitoris as he massaged his manhood until he was satisfied. Then he whispered, "Sweet dreams princess."

I felt confused and disgusting. I waited until the sun rose before, I raced to the shower. I scrubbed my body thoroughly as I let the water blend in with my tears. As I left the bathroom, my mother was coming in from work.

"Ma, can I talk to you?"

"Yeah, sure. Wassup?"

"In the room please."

"Come on now. What's up?" She responded, apparently annoyed. I followed her in the room quickly. "What's wrong?" She asked before looking at me. I closed Lee's room door behind us.

"Grandpop came in my room last night and touched my stuff." I pointed to my vagina as I began, and her entire body tensed up. Before I could continue, her phone rang.

"Hey babe!" She said in the receiver when she answered. "No, I'm not busy. I was just thinking about you. Are we still on Miami this weekend?" She continued on with her conversation for about ten more minutes.

"Maaaa." I whined in disbelief that she actually disregarded me to answer the phone for one of her many men.

"Hold on Baby," she said annoyed obviously. "What Diamond?"

"I just told you what Ma." I said frustrated.

"Are you sure? It probably was a bad dream. I used to have those. Push your totes up against your door at night and let me know if it happens again." She went back to her conversation as if what I was telling her wasn't important. So, I began questioning the importance myself. Was this normal? It couldn't be because it wouldn't feel so nasty and disgusting if it was.

"Maaa."

"Look. I told you what to fucking do. If that ain't good enough, go tell Mae. This is her house. Let her handle it." I stood frozen in the moment, hurt, and lost to my own thoughts. I thought about going down the hall and telling my Grandmother but what would she say? Would she believe me? I went back to my room and found a fifty-dollar bill on my dresser. As I picked it up, Lilly came in my room.

"Damn! Your Dad gave you that?"

"Naw. The devil." Lilly laughed but her laughter died down when she realized my face was serious.

"What's wrong? Talk to me." As I was about to say something, Grandpop knocked at my room door heavy.

"Get y'all asses' downstairs to breakfast." He shouted.

"Nothing." I replied to Lilly. "You can have that money. Split it with Porsha and make sure that y'all get Lee, Trina, and Isis a few things too."

"Are you sure you're okay?" Lilly asked concerned.

"I never said I was." I said silently.

That was the primary reason why, at this point, I vowed to myself to get my life in order. No one else would ever raise my daughter. I will always be in the position to protect and provide for her. Just as I was popping it to Destiny's Child's Christmas Medley, there was a knock at my door. Pete was the only person I was expecting, but he had a key, so it had to be them hard head ass sisters of mine. I told them that I wanted them to commit to being with their families for Christmas. Since I was released from the hospital, they had been by my side day in and day out. I finished putting the turkey bacon on the pan and slid it into the toaster oven quickly and sat the pancakes on the table.

Knock! Knock! Knock!

"Oh Shit! The door." I wobbled over to the door. I looked out the peephole at Lilly and Porsha. "What did I tell you bitches?" I asked as I snatched the door open and blocked them from entering my apartment.

"Bitch, if you don't get your big ass out of the way! Your ass can't cook bitch so we're coming to feed our mother fucking niece." Porsha screamed loudly.

"We just want to feed you. That's all. We'll leave afterwards." Lilly said softly while giving Porsha the side eye.

"Pete is on his way & y'all know he doesn't celebrate holidays so none of that Christmas decorations stuff."

"If you get the fuck out of our way, we can get started. The sooner we get started, the sooner we can leave bitch." Porsha flashed a fake smile as she looked around me. She sniffed. "Your ass already in here burning up the turkey bacon. How do you burn turkey bacon? The shit is practically rubber?" They were right. I could not cook. In fact, Pete and I planned on ordering in. He was bringing his son, Sharif, over but he was on formula and baby cereal, so he was safe from my attempt at breakfast. Plus, I'm sure Pete would be pleased to have a home cooked meal that he didn't have to cook himself. I walked away from the door and plopped down on my plush couch. Lilly sat her bags on the counter, then came & plopped next to me.

"It is so beautiful in here. I would've never imagined this coordination but leave it up to you to bless it with your skills." She said and laid her head on my shoulders.

"Girl, it was all boredom and Pinterest." We giggled. Silence followed our giggles and I dozed off for about 30 minutes before I heard another knock at the door. I attempted to get up, but Lilly instructed me to stay put as she opened the door for Pete. "Why didn't you use your key?" I asked.

"As you can see, my hands are full babe. Can you grab him?" I wiggled my way free of my soft couch and unstrapped Sharif from his car seat. I kissed his soft chunky cheeks as I picked him up and held him close as I smelled him. I loved the way babies smelled. Talking baby talk to him, he smiled as we made my way to our favorite spot, my comfortable bed. "Thanks, beautiful!" Pete exhaled causing me to blush.

I loved how Pete always complimented me. The part I loved most is that I knew in my heart that he meant it. He liberated my esteem even though I felt like a big fat whale. I was ready for my baby girl to come on. I could not wait to kiss and hug on her while talking baby talk, but for now I had my chunky baby Reef, as we called him. Pete excused himself and went in the bathroom to shower and change into his house clothes. We all talked and laughed for a bit before I cuddled up with Reef, singing him to sleep. One he dozed off, I got up and headed into the kitchen area to get a plate because I was starving.

"What's stopping you from forgiving Pete?" Lilly asked. Caught off guard by her question, I paused for a moment to think about it as I usually made it my business to suppress those types of thoughts. I didn't know what was stopping me from forgiving Pete, whom in comparison to others I'd forgiven easily for worst things, surely deserved my forgiveness. It had been ten years since we lost Malik and doctors confirmed there was no foul play. Not that I thought that there had been. Devon just had my mind so gone at that time, he planted different thoughts in my head that made my guard go up with Pete for years. Malik died from Sudden Infant Death Syndrome. The autopsy, that I got against Pete's wishes, determined that. Also, I still resented the fact that though we both loss our son, Pete was afforded the blessing of experiencing his last moments of life. Pete loved Malik with his entire being and I know he'd never hurt him, but as a mother I often wonder if something more could have been done to save my baby. Losing Malik made me lose my entire mind. I shivered thinking back to those times.

"Have you ever lost a child?" I asked. Lilly took the food out the oven and sat her oven mitts on the counter.

"No, but I do know that regardless of your shortcomings, GOD has forgiven you time and time again and is continuously blessing you. Pete is one of those blessings. Why not extend him some grace? He deserves to be forgiven. If GOD can forgive, why can't you? You are not better than GOD, are you? That is the last time I am going to say anything about it. I just want you to appreciate what you have before it's gone." Lilly said and threw her hands up like in a manner of surrender.

"Alright. It is time for y'all to go. Thanks for the meal but I can handle it from here." I said jokingly.

"Bitch, you would put us out once we're done cooking and ain't shit to handle except opening the damn rolls." Porsha said as she laughed.

"You know me so well." I smiled. Putting my nose in the middle of the fresh daisies that Pete had placed in my flower vase upon coming in, I smiled. He kept fresh flowers in my vase, and it was the most thoughtful thing that anyone has ever done for me. Reaching into the cabinet, I pulled out a twenty-piece glass bowl set that I had bought when I moved in. I never thought I would use it because Pete never cooked enough for us to have leftovers. My mouth watered as I helped them away pack my favorites; barbeque chicken, roast beef, macaroni and cheese, corn, mashed potatoes, salmon cakes, caesar salad, spinach, cornbread, and deviled eggs. "Y'all are the best man. I swear." I said hugging them. Pete's phone rung and after a short conversation, he went in the bathroom and changed back into his clothes. I continued to indulge in conversation with my sisters, but I was watching his every move.

"Excuse me ladies. I gotta make a run D. Can you hold it down for me?" Pete asked referring to Reef.

"Don't I always?" I said with an attitude. Not because I had a problem watching Reef. I was upset that every time he promised to spend an entire day with us, something always came up. It never failed. Reef & I would always be left to enjoy our day alone. Whatever though. At least Reef enjoyed my company.

"I can stay here with you if you want Sis. I don't have anything else to do. Plus, I can help you with Sharif." Lilly offered.

"Yeah and McKenzie is over Lee's house with the girls, so I can stay too bitch. But we are not dealing with that funky ass pregnancy attitude." I glared at Pete. I was two weeks away from my due date and my baby could come at any time. I knew being a business owner came with a high demand on time, especially since he was holding everything down by himself, so I tried not to complain. It seemed like the further along I got into my pregnancy, the more frustrated I got with the lack of time spent. Often, I tried hard to keep in the fore front that he was not my man and that he did more than enough to take care of me. I was still working at the center, but my boss insisted that I take my maternity leave at 37 weeks because my feet were starting to hurt severely. He assured me that I could come back after being cleared by the doctor post pregnancy. So, I relaxed most days. Drug court still required that I went to at least two meetings a week until I went into labor. So, Pete had been taking me to my meetings since my feet hurt too bad to drive too.

"Cool Beans." I smiled. I had not spent time with them since Thanksgiving, so I was excited. I knew Porsha had all the hood gossip since I was not able to go outside.

"Thanks sisters!" Pete kissed my forehead. "I'll bring you some ice cream when I come back." He said trying to butter me up. He kissed my forehead as I rolled my eyes.

"Thank you." I replied and smiled reluctantly.

I got each of them a night gown so they could sit on my bed with me because I didn't like outside clothes on my bed. I was on bed rest according to Pete, so I hadn't been outside in about a month. So, I was ready to gossip with Porsha while Lilly judged us. Porsha & I loved the excitement of the streets, while Lilly was more reserved. She was married to a hustler but that's as far as it went though. She had her master's in Business Administration and owned her own real estate business flipping houses. She stayed buried in work and liked to know as less as possible about what her husband or any other hustler did in their line of business. Porsha & I were not like Lilly in that way. After we all ate and fed Reef, Porsha & Lilly changed, and we all got comfortable on the bed. I turned on soft jazz music which soon put Sharif to sleep.

"Bitch spill the tea!" I shrieked.

"Where do I start bitchhhh?" Porsha said happily.

"Wherever. Just give me some life because right now, Love and Hip Hip is the only excitement I have and waiting a week between episodes is killing me."

"Welllllll...the Baltimore edition is so much better. For starters, you know Devon had the Milton Ave strip locked down before he got locked up. A few weeks before he got booked though, it was already some new niggas moving in on the territory on the Biddle Street part. Word is every day them niggas was beefing. They lost a few niggas and Devon lost a few niggas. It was like the usual back and forth beef with niggas but this time every day someone was dropping though!" Porsha explained to me as Lilly played her word game on her phone completely unentertained by our conversation.

"Damn, but they ain't kill his ugly ass?"

"Same thing I said bitch!" Porsha agreed.

"Y'all are terrible." Lilly shook her head.

"Okayyy Deaconess Lilly Sue." I said and we fell out laughing. "Go head SG. What else happened bitch?" I turned my attention back to Porsha.

"Rick, the nigga Devon was beefing with, is a big-time hustler from North Carolina. So, with the Feds running down on Devon's niggas and swiping them up. He moved in with no problem. He lost some niggas but ultimately, he won the battle and they said he had shit bumping out that bitch too. He was taking business from all the surrounding neighborhoods."

"Was? What happened?"

"What you think? He got killed. You know you can't get too much money in this city. Especially not coming from another state."

"Whattttt??!! That's crazy for real."

"Yesssssss bitch but not by none of Devon's bitch ass niggas that was still on the streets. Them niggas waved the white flag once they saw them niggas wasn't playing. Practically gave the nigga their blocks. Within two weeks – just two weeks bitch – that nigga Rick had Milton Ave strip tied the fuck up from Milton and Lanvale all the way down to Milton and Ashland."

"So, I'm confused. If Devon niggas ain't tag him then who did?"

"Calm down bitch. I'm boutta tell you!" Porsha screwed her face up and rolled her eyes at my impatience.

"D, you need to calm down before you have my niece early." Lilly said and turned her attention back to her game. Porsha and I both rolled our eyes at her ass.

"Anywayyyy," Porsha as she rolled her eyes. "They said he tried to stretch that bitch all the way down to the bottom by Monument & Milton, but the nigga Dollar Bill wasn't having it. Dollar Bill was making a few moves before he got booked; nothing too major but word is that the nigga a hitter and that's what really laced his pockets. Well, Dollar Bill just came home, and he got the box strip right there, Monument to Jefferson and Milton to Luzerne. So, when Rick tried his little stunt, it didn't go well. Needless to say, he was burying two more of his niggas. They said that nigga Dollar Bill put a halt to that shit immediately. Ain't play around with them niggas either. Then, literally went straight for Rick. Caught his ass slipping in some pussy – like most big niggas get hit – and got his ass out of here. Then went on about his day like ain't shit happen. I was like damn I'm scared a little bit. Can I safely get a chicken box out of Pandas? Shat!"

"I know right! I was sitting here like damn. Is it weird that it turns me on a bit?"

"Yes!" Lilly said with her face displaying disgust. Porsha & I laughed.

"Bitch no because I was like I want to see him in person. Not on no trynna holla at him shit but I just wanna put the face to the name." Porsha continued.

"Trueeee. Nigga scare me and intrigue at the same time." I thought. The way Porsha talks about him reminded me of my father before his alcoholism took over him.

"Bitch, exactly! But on to the next tea. I ran into Shymeek and we were rapping a little, but he already knew my rap for him was limited because of that fuck shit his sister pulled with Devon. That ain't stop him from spilling the tea though."

"Oh Lord. What did he have to say because you know he stay mixed up in some shit?"

"It wasn't about him. It was about Meka."

"What about her?" I asked.

"He was like Meka and Devon been fighting and beefing and shit. More than likely him fighting on her. But one day while they were beefing, she told him that he's mad that you're having a baby and he blew up on her and beat her so bad he broke some of her ribs. They haven't been back together since then. He cut her off completely financially and put her and the baby out his house. Ain't that some dumb shit?"

"He really gotta get over it yo. I don't get him. I did any and everything for that nigga. Loved him more than my own self and what did I get in return? Physical abuse, sexual abuse, mental abuse, emotional abuse, disrespect, embarrassment, disloyalty, shot at, kidnapped, and locked up in treatment like a fucking junkie. Like damn. Move around nigga."

"What do you mean sexual abuse? Like rape? He raped you?" Lilly asked concerned.

"I don't know what to call it but I just remember nights when I would get fucked up – I mean fucked up and pass out – he would still fuck me even though I wasn't awake." I started and Lilly gasped. "One time, he drugged me and said I wouldn't have taken it willingly and he was just trying to show me a good time. How if I was incoherent?"

"Incoherent?" Porsha asked confused.

"Yes, incoherent. I wouldn't be awake to know what's going on. The morning after or later on in the day – depending on when i would come to – I would be in pain and my pussy would be sore. Then, I'd have cum coming out of my pussy when I urinate. My nipples would be sore and tender to touch. All of that and I would not even remember the encounter. I'd say something to him about it and he would say things like

'You're my woman and you wouldn't deny me sex so why is it a problem?' and he would really believe that shit to be excusable. He would tell me I'm tripping and shit. Then the love bombing would happen. He'd buy me a bunch of stuff or take me on a trip and think I swept it under the rug and was okay. Honestly, I was never okay, but I didn't want to go back home so, i don't know.. .maybe, I made myself believe what he was saying to be true. But I never felt okay. It honestly made me feel like when Grandpop used to touch me." The tears begin to flow from Lilly's eyes as we all sat there in silence for a few minutes. Porsha and I grabbed her and held her close and my own tears started to find their way down my cheeks. Grandpop abused me for almost a year before I couldn't take it anymore. I told Porsha and Lilly and together, we told Grandma Mae. Grandpop passed a day or two later. They found his body floating in the Inner Harbor. We all knew what happened, but we never talked about it. Grandma Mae cremated him and tossed his ashes. He had a pretty hefty life insurance policy that she cashed in on and we lived off for years until she met Mr. Kevin who was a breath of fresh air compared to Grandpop. Lilly always felt bad that she didn't protect me but over the years I tried to assure her that I never felt that way and that we had to move forward.

"I'm so sorry D." Lilly said through her sobs while wiping the tears from her face. "I'm really sorry. I always fail at protecting you. I am your big sister. I'm supposed to bear the pain for you."

"Lillianne, relax. That shit they did ain't on you. It is on them. They are the predators. I am just saying Devon fucked me over in ways unimaginable; exhausting any chance he could have at rekindling anything with me. I should have been done with him. But how does the saying go? Better late than never. Fuck them. And definitely fuck him. Why does it matter if I am having a baby? It's been months and I haven't had any contact with him. Changed phones and my phone number without reaching out to him at all so he should know he doesn't have shit coming with me. "

"You made him believe he always could come back. Repeatedly forgiving him no matter what he did to you. You have an issue with that. You are too understanding; always trying to rationalize someone's inexcusable behaviors. Always feeling like you can fix something no matter how broken it becomes. You have never been good at letting go. Most times, you won't let go no matter how much it hurts until the other party forces you to." Lilly spoke softly.

"Shymeek also said that Devon is very adamant about finding out who your child's father is. He's been asking around and trying to get your contact information. He even stopped pass Aunt Babs house but she wasn't there and you know Uncle Chink or Reef wasn't going to tell him shit. Sooner or later, he will find out though." Porsha said jumping back into the gossip but I was over it.

"Well, it's surely not a secret but you know how private Pete is so that's probably why he doesn't know yet. But Fuck Devon. fuck him. I hope he does find out. Maybe, he'll have a heart attack and die. What else?" I rolled my eyes and Porsha laughed.

"The tea just warming up bitch. Meka is homeless."

"What you mean homeless? You mean to tell me that she ain't have no bread put up?"

"What bread bitch? Shymeek said that nigga never gave her a bitch ass penny. He just took care of her, the baby, and the bills, but never gave her any money for herself. So, anything she needed, had to go through him and he would get it for her. Then he said that Devon would always play like he so stretched thin money wise and of course she went for that shit. Now, we all know that nigga got money he sitting on somewhere. One thing that nigga is not is broke. Plus, they said he only looking at doing seven years, so you know he got some money tucked somewhere for after he knock that out. Plus the nigga has a documented history of mental health issues so that's going to knock some of that time down too. You know he'll work the system."

"That's fucked up. That girl got a baby to take care of."

"Yup. He doesn't give a fuck though. He put her in a fucked up living situation with their baby and still keeps telling her he's broke. I'm talking about the girl is on the street, staying place to place homeless with the infant. She goes to the rec when it opens in the morning until it closes at night, begging and shit. The word is she had treated Ms. Ann and the rest of the fam like shit while she was with him so they ain't fucking with her. It's sad but you know what they say, karma doesn't miss a beat. She had to know that no good would come from fucking him."

"Damn. So, she's homeless with the baby?" I asked concerned. No, I didn't fuck with Meka, but I'd never want to see anyone experience homelessness with their child. "That's Devon for you! Trifling ass nigga. Make you hooked to him and leave you hanging. Nigga loved looking like more money than he had but you can't bet your last dollar that he is going to keep some money put up for himself. Selfish ass petty ass grimey ass bitch ass nigga. Just fucking pathetic." I shook my head in disgust. No child should have to suffer based on the poor decisions of their parents. I know Devon was taking care of Meka really good in the beginning. That's what he does. That's how he gains control of you. He chooses young and naive girls, provides them with a lifestyle beyond what their small minds could imagine to be normal. He would buy them whatever they wanted, take them on trips, and keep them fly, so that when he said he wanted something, they'd feel obligated to do it. I know because I was one of those young girls. Difference between me and them is I always saved something in the kitty. Even if it was only a few thousand dollars. Anything was better than nothing. No matter what situation I was in and no matter how secure I felt, I always put something up for a rainy day like my grandmother taught me as a kid.

"That's what her ass gets. She ain't give a fuck about your feelings. Fuck that dick eating ass bitch. Are you getting soft on me bitch?"

"It's called empathy not sympathy bitch. I have no sympathy whatsoever for that hoe, but I would hope that if the situation presented itself as mine, someone feel for me and my kid the same way."

"Okayyy! Next topic because I'm not feeling your aura around this conversation to the point that it's pissing me off." Porsha said smugly and I laughed until my stomach hurt. My siblings were so protective over me and my feelings. I appreciated it but I firmly believe you attract the energy you project. I made a mental note to call my job in the morning and see if we had any openings for our Women with Children program.

"Something is wrong with you!" I shouted while still laughing.

"Duh, your mother smoked weed while she was carrying me bitch. Clouded my soft spot." Porsha responded. We snickered as she looked over at Lilly who had fallen asleep. "Lilly! Lilly!" Porsha called out to her, but Lilly didn't respond. She was knocked out.

"She's sleep bitch. Leave her alone." I said.

"Good. Let me hurry up before she gets up. Charisma called me a couple weeks ago asking about you, but I let him know that you were on bed rest because you were about to burst out a baby girl. Of course, he sent his congratulations and well wishes, but he still wanted to discuss business. So, I went and met with him. He wants us to get the girls together again. I told him you were about to drop so you couldn't right now but I'm sure the gang is gonna feel like me, we're not doing it without you." Charisma was a nigga that we'd met in a night club when we traveled to Philadelphia for a celebration. He flirted with Porsha but once she told him she was married, he slid her his card and informed her to call him if she wanted to make some money. We ain't know what type of shit he was on so we ran the information by Aunt Babs and Aunt Shelly who used to own a strip club together in Philly and they happened to use to know his father. They had known Charisma's family to be into drugs and brothels so they warned us to be careful. Of course, we still reached out to see what it was about. It turned out being a drug transporting business opportunity and against my better judgement, we hopped on board. Porsha and I rounded up our closest friends and went all for a good eight months until Charisma got knocked off. Thankfully he was a solid nigga or we all would have been in jail. Beneficially for him, the state had a weak case and his lawyer ate their asses up, so he was able to beat it. He chilled out after that, but I guess he was back to the paper now.

"I'm done with that shit. I got a little that girl now. It's not just me anymore. Niggas is catching football numbers behind drug cases now. I can't risk leaving my daughter and neither can you."

"True but we are not them. We are smart. Bitch, you are the smartest. It is because of you that everything ran like it did. Are we both good drivers? Yes, but you are also a good leader and organizer as well a quick thinker. Like when we were in tight situations, it was your brain that kept us from behind bars. You are like a fucking genius for real. I mean if you don't want to do this shit, you still need to start a business or something. You have the skill set to build an empire. Either that or work for a bookkeeping business. Look, something bitch. I don't know. Some people are just natural born hustlers. You're one of those people. Pete takes good care of you, but I know you miss getting your own money and having your independence. I know you do."

"Porsh. I love you and I love how you think the world of me. Bitch, I'm forever going to love getting money and I am going to figure out a way to get to it. However, my situation is different now. I'm about to have a healthy baby girl despite me being undeserving. You have a kid bitch. We are mothers. We can't fuck with it. Plus, shit has changed. It's a different game being played out there." I reasoned.

"All I'm saying is think about it." Porsha said with her hands up.

"There's nothing to think about. I ain't fucking with it."

"Respect." Porsha said as she rolled her eyes and an eerie silence filled the air.

"Y'all can still do it. I'll be the assistant or something." Lilly said.

"Bitchhhh! I knew your ass wasn't sleep." Porsha said.

"I was but it's hard to stay sleep with your big ass mouth."

"Anyway, if D out, I'm out. I'm not riding with anybody else. You already know. We gotta come up with a way to get some money though this 9-5 ain't cutting for me."

"Stop buying so many damn wigs." Lilly retarted and I almost fell out from laughing so hard.

"Never bitch!" Porsha laughed.

"I'll think of something. What else is new? What's happening on the Avenue?

"Bitchhhhh. . ." Porsha started and just like that we talked for hours. We caught up on everything. She brought me up to date on everybody's business and some of her own. She caught me up with my grandmother and how she was doing. From the sounds of things, she was happy and worry free. She deserved that. I missed her so much, but my guilt would not allow me to call her and say it verbally. I wasn't ready to hear my well-deserved lecture. We laughed, cried, plotted, planned, and played with Reef until we all fell asleep. Shortly after, Pete came to take Reef home. Porsha and Lilly dressed to leave as well. He asked if I wanted to ride but I declined. I showered and turned on some music so that I could get some rest. Tossing and turning, I couldn't get comfortable enough to fall asleep. Suddenly, I heard my grandmother's voice clear as day, 'When you can't sleep, talk to GOD.' So, I prayed.

Dear GOD,

I am so grateful for everything that you've done for me. I'm asking you to cover my family and my friends, Lord. Cover Meka and her baby Lord. I don't know what tomorrow holds for me but please order my footsteps. Remove any malice from my heart allow me to help operate from a genuine place. You have saved myself and my baby from some hurdles and hardships. Help me pay it forward. In your name I pray,

AMEN!

Chapter Seven

Bright and early, I was up and out with my first stop being my job. I attempted to call several times, but I knew first had how hard it was to keep the front desk staffed with volunteers and mornings were always chaotic. It was also the day after Christmas, so I assumed everyone was still relaxed, which was fine, but it was the beginning of Winter and it was already very cold. I was determined to get Meka some place warm and stable to stay for the sake of her baby. So, I got dressed and made my way. The ride there was long and a bit uncomfortable, but I made it. I checked the clock on the dashboard and saw that it was only 8:40am. The executives didn't get in until 9:00am so I decided to wait in the car. I leaned my head on the car door and shut my eyes but my phone rung before I could drift off to sleep. Picking up the phone, I saw it was Pete.

"Are you okay?" he asked as soon as I accepted the call.

"Yes. I just had something important to handle."

"You had an appointment?"

"No. Just had to run an errand. That's all. I didn't think to call and let you know that I wasn't going to be in the house this morning. My apologies."

"I was about to say I ain't have nothing written in my book for today but as long as you and baby girl are okay, I'm great. Next time, a call or even a text would be nice though. You know how I am. I came to bring you breakfast. I'll leave it in the microwave and take your trash out. Do you need me to leave you anything? Or bring you dinner tonight though?"

"I don't need anything, but dinner sounds lovely. Thanks baby daddy. Can you stay with me tonight too?"

"Yes, I can. Are you sure you're alright though?" he asked concerned. I had to even ask myself. I was not usually very mushy, but I was overly emotional that day. I looked up and saw Ms. Erin going up the stairs to go into the building. "

Yes, I'm good. Gotta go. See you tonight." Before he could respond, I hung up. I hopped out of the car and made my way to the bottom of the building's steps. "Ms. E! Hold up. I need your help please!"

"Don't tell me your ass is about to go into labor Diamond!" She responded. Out of breath, I paused to laugh.

"I am not going into labor. I need you though. Please tell me you have a spot in the women with children program."

"Diamond, you relapsed again?" She asked disappointedly.

"Oh nooo. It's not for me."

"Oh okay. I'm sorry. We're full right now." She said as she unlocked the door to the building.

"I need you to make a space." I said and my voice cracked. She turned around and looked me in my eyes. Not sure if it was the baby screwing up my hormones or my heart, but my emotions were kicking it up to overdrive. "I know a young lady who is sleeping pillar to post right now with an infant. Please Ms. E."

"Bring her here in the morning. Nine o'clock AM sharp Diamond. If she's not here, that's it!" I cried as I breathed a sigh of relief. "Alright. Alright with the mushy shit." Ms. E said with a screw face. Everyone was surprised by my heightened emotions.

"Thank you. She'll be here." I wobbled back to the car. My next stop was Oliver Recreation Center or "The Rec" as we called it. As I drove across North Avenue, I turned my music on and bopped my head as my 90s R&B playlist on Pandora took me down memory lane. My phone rang again, and I already knew it was Pete.

"Hey handsome." I answered the phone.

"Don't hey handsome me. Are you okay?"

"Yes, I'm fine. I went to talk to the CEO of my job about her new women with children program for a friend."

"For who? Porsha?"

"That's my sister. I said my friend."
"Well, you don't have any friends."

"You don't know what I have." I said annoyed.

"If you need space or desire to revive your independence, just say that. You do not have to move to a program for space. Just let..."

"What the fuck are you talking about? I told you I'm fine and I told you what the fuck I'm doing. Why would I ask you to come stay the night with me if getting space from you was my motive for handling business today? Look, you are tripping and I'm not in the mood for you. Let's not forget that you are not my fucking man Pete." He hung up and I chuckled. I turned my phone on DND.

Funny how men claimed it was women who were always in their feelings. Here I was trying to do some good in the world and a nigga in his feelings thinking I'm moving funny. I pulled on the side of The Rec and sat in the car for a minute. It was funny how life worked. Here I was trying to save a woman who assisted the man I loved in ripping my heart to pieces. However, one thing I learned from attending my narcotics anonymous meetings was that when you help someone else, you're helping yourself more. I know Porsha was somewhere cussing me out like crazy, but Lilly would be proud of me, so I focused on Lilly's energy. Smiling, I hopped out my car and made my way into the building. As I opened the door to the gym, I could hear my cousin Sissy cussing the coaches out because her son wasn't getting enough game time. We hugged, and she kissed my belly before going right back to cussing and fussing. I looked around and spotted Meka in the corner with her backed turned. I was sure she saw me come in and probably turned around so I wouldn't see her. Shit, I understood. I would react the same way if I was in her shoes. I could feel people's eyes on me as I made my way to her. When I came to her, I stopped. Frustration was written all over her face as she rocked her baby attempting to quiet her crying.

"May I try?" I asked extending my arms. She looked up at me with hesitation.

"Girl, I'm not going to do anything to hurt your baby. I would fuck you up. But your baby? Never." She handed me the baby. After I sat down in the chair next to Meka, I rocked baby girl while humming to her. I could hear Meka breathe a sigh of relief to hear the baby stop wailing. I looked at the baby as I soothed her. She was so beautiful. Her chocolate skin and deep curly locks of hair reminded me of her father and a single tear forced itself from my eye. Quickly, I wiped the tear away. I heard Meka's stomach growl. At first, I screwed my face up but then I gathered myself quickly.

"Get y'all stuff together. Let's go." I demanded and Meka looked at me confused, looked around, and then back at me but did not speak. "Look, I can hear your fucking stomach growling louder than the damn basketball bouncing." I said in a low tone. "I'm two weeks away from being due. What the fuck can I possibly do to you or your baby without risking mine?"

"What's your motives?"

"Helping your baby. If I was in your shoes, I would hope that someone would help me and my baby the same. That does not change the fact that I do not fuck with you. I care about your daughter being safe. Especially since she is subject to living conditions that are outside of her control. This ain't about you at all."

"Hmmm. Naw. I don't need your help. I'm good. You just want to help so you can say you did; making me look even worse of a person that I already do. Giving everybody something else to talk about."

"I have no choice but to respect your decision, but you aren't good. I do not have to give anyone ammunition to talk about you. You do well with that on your own. Do you think this is about revenge? Because if so, you are sadly mistaken. I allow GOD to handle the karma of the ones that fuck me over. And from my position, it seems like he is already taught you your lesson. It's cold in here. At least let me take you to get some food in a warm environment." She held her head down and more tears fell. "Don't cry. This is not a pity party. Come on." She gathered up all of her belongings and we exited The Rec. Of course, there were whispers but I was used to that. Mother fuckers talked about me my entire life, so my chin was up as I wobbled out. I instructed her to put her bags in the trunk as she strapped the baby's car seat in. We got in my car and I drove to Texas Roadhouse. Our ride was silent outside of the sounds of DMX's voice serenading through the speakers. Once we got to the diner, I grabbed the baby bag while she grabbed the baby. We settled in and ordered drinks while she scraped the formula container to prepare the baby a bottle before tapping the last bit of cereal in there. "Is that the last of her food?"

"Yeah." She replied barely above a whisper.

"Look, I'm not here to hurt you, to be spiteful, or cause you any issues. Devon is a foul nigga to have his kid out here living like this. I don't respect that. You're a grown ass woman but that baby is innocent. I know you don't have anywhere stable to stay so I got you a spot at my job. If you want it. There, you and your baby will have a stable space. It's an apartment share community so you'll share an apartment with 1-2 other roommates, but you'll have your own furnished room with cable television. There are rules though." Her face lit up as I talked, and her tears flowed without restriction.

"As long as my baby has a consistent, safe space to lay her head, I'll abide by any rules they have."

"Good. Most importantly, it doesn't matter if you have anything in your system now. You cannot drink or do any drugs while you are in there. If there is anything in your system already, they have to see that your levels are going down or else they will put your ass out and there is nothing I can do to save you from that."

"I promise I'm not going to fuck up. I've been saying that I would go into a shelter but my pride..." She stopped talking and put her head down.

"Look, when it comes to your kid, you gotta suck that pride shit up! Being a mother comes first. I'm not one of those people who will tell you that I don't care what people think of me because I do but you never let a mother fucker see that. You do whatever you gotta do for your baby with your head held high. Because believe me, when it comes to this one," I pointed to my belly. "It's no limit to what I'll do to make sure she never has a worry."

"I'm not strong like you D."

"Yes, you are. Everyone has stength necessary for their battles. GOD said so and who is HE to lie? You just have to tap into that strength."

"I've never been strong."

"Well bitch! You don't have a choice now. You're a fucking mother now! So, all that pity party shit, get the fuck over it. Nobody owes you shit but you and you owe your baby girl everything. You ain't gonna get it until you put your big girl panties on. You can cry all you need to. I will cry every got damn day, but I'm still gotta shake and move. Look at your beautiful daughter. Let her be your peace in this storm. Let her be your reason why. Focus on what you want for her and everything else is going to fall into place."

"You're right."

"I know. I ain't gonna tell you shit that I wouldn't advise myself."

"I know." She responded and we paused talking for a minute to order food. Afterwards, we talked and laughed and caught up on our families and how they were doing. She apologized several times, but I let her know that the only apology I needed was for her to get on her shit for her baby. I do not know if it was because I was finally outside or because I was actually enjoying myself, but I felt good; like on the inside. It felt good to be in position to help someone else. Our food came, and we ate in silence. I was stuffed, and my baby girl was super active. We chatted lightly to allow our food to digest before leaving. Our next stop was the market. Too full to get out, I pulled right in front of the market. I gave Meka a hundred-dollar bill and told her get the baby a big can of formula and whatever baby food she enjoyed. I also told her grab herself some stuff. She looked back at her baby hesitantly.

"Girl, if you don't go get that damn milk. We ain't going nowhere. Your baby is safe with me Meka." She looked back again at her sleeping baby before exiting the car. I didn't feel like parking so against the warning sign that was in front of me, I put on my emergency blinkers. After about 20 minutes, Meka came out with a few bags and got back in the car. An obvious look of relief spread across her face as she began to realize that my intentions were pure. Shifting to drive, I pulled off in route to our next destination, Walmart. Now, I don't care how tired I was, how full I was, or how bad my feet hurt, I was going in Walmart. Thankfully it was a motorized cart at the entrance. We traveled straight to the baby section and I loaded my cart down with more stuff for my baby girl even though she didn't need anything else. I handed Meka two one hundred-dollar bills and advised she get what her and her baby needed. We spent every bit of two hours in Walmart. Just talking and browsing. After loading down the trunk, we settled into the car. It was a cold night and I was exhausted.

"Do you have some place safe to stay for the night?"

"Not really but we can stay at Murder's girlfriend's house. She usually let us crash on her couch." Murder was her baby brother who I just learned last night from Porsha was on the run and was still dealing drugs out of that girl's house. I knew her staying there with her baby could put them both at risk, so I tried to think of who I knew that would let her crash at their place. My mind immediately went to my grandmother. She would take in anyone in need, but she was all the way in South Carolina, and I still hadn't talked to her and it seemed like forever. My guilt really hadn't allowed me to pick up the phone.

"When is the last time you slept in a bed?"

"It's been a minute honestly."

"Cool. You're going to sleep in a one tonight." I drove them to Red Roof Inn & Suites. I got her a room and left her my contact numbers with instructions on being ready by 8am. I left after helping her get situated and just sat in the car. I was extremely tired, and my eyes were so heavy. I decided to call Pete and see if he could pick me up, but I opened my phone to several messages from him. The most important one read 'We need to talk'. I thought great because we could talk on my way in. I called him; no answer. I called him a few times more, and still no answer. I decided to get a room for myself because I didn't want to risk driving. I grabbed one of my new night gowns, underwear, and slippers from the trunk and proceeded to the front desk. I looked around because I had that eerie feeling of being watched again. I did a complete circle just to check all my surroundings. Nothing seemed out of place. I hit my car alarm again just to be sure I secured it. Once I checked in, I went immediately to my room. I picked up my phone to call Pete as I sat down on the toilet to urinate, but he was already calling me.

"Where have you been all day?" he asked before I could get a chance to say hello.

"Out handling some business. I told you that. Why didn't you answer the phone? Anything could've been wrong with me!"

"Mannn I've been calling you all day Diamond. Miss me with that dumb shit. What type of games are you playing? You're due in two weeks and you're out driving and shit knowing you are not supposed to. You asked me to come stay with you, but I've been here for a minute and you haven't gotten here yet."

"Pete, who the fuck said I couldn't drive? You? You are not my fucking doctor. I am fine. I was hoping to call you to feel better because I have had a long day, but I see you just want to make my headache worst. So, you enjoy your night and don't call my fucking phone back tonight." I hung up and sat my alarm for 7am. I took of my clothes and wobbled into the shower. I showered until my skin felt wrinkled. I slipped on my nightgown and laid down. The bed was comfortable causing me to fall asleep almost instantly. After a long day and arguing with Pete, I was happy that at least my dream was good to me.

I sat under a tree with my baby girl in my lap. She was so beautiful. She looked just like Pete's mother. I smiled and kissed her face. As I turned around so that I can see the face of the great smelling gentleman who was holding my waist firmly, my dream began to fade. All I could see was his beautiful smile and his smooth butter brown skin. Just as I turned my head back to my baby girl, I looked down to realize I was pregnant again. My baby girl giggled as she said, "Baby Mommy Baby." I woke up to the phone ringing and of course, it was Pete.

Chapter Eight

"Whatttt?!" I screamed into the phone as I picked it up without even looking at the caller ID. I knew it had to be one of my sisters because they are the only ones who called my house phone.

"Happy New Year Bitchhhhhhhhhhhh!" Porsha screamed into the phone. I hung up the phone. My phone rang again. This time I exhaled loudly as I answered the phone. "Tell my niece Happy New Year too. And fuck you bitch." This time she hung up. I laughed so hard it hurt. I loved my baby girl, but I was beyond ready for her to get out of me. I was miserable. Everything in my body hurt from the top of my head to the bottom of my feet. I had been in bed mostly since I got home from taking Meka and her baby girl to the program. Outside of taking a shower, eating, and urinating, I didn't get out my bed for anything. It hurt too bad to. Lilly had been staying with me during the days to take care of me. I had to convince her to go out and have fun tonight. Hearing the front door broke me from my thoughts. Unable to turn around, I heard Pete turning the key. I hadn't talked to Pete since that night we fussed on the phone when I was at the hotel and I hadn't realized how much I missed him. In fact, I called him once when I got home, but he didn't answer. I didn't bother to call back either. The pain I was in left no energy for me to cater to his feelings about dumb shit.

"D, you sleep?" he asked as he turned the light on.

"If I was, I'm not now." He knew I hated light. Instantly, I went from missing him to wanting him to go right the fuck back out the door.

"We need to talk."

"What is it Peter Newman?" I snapped as I stayed in the same position. I was in pain and did not have time to play with him. He paused for a minute.

"Can I lay with you?" He asked. As bad as I wanted to still be mad with him, I was in pain and wanted to be held so my attitude softened.

"Of course. Can you help me get up so I can get on my side?"

"You can stay there. I can get on the other side."

"Thanks, because my back hurts like hell. I really didn't want to get up." He turned the light off and walked around the bed. I admired his shadow. I closed my eyes, but I felt him stop and stare at me before climbing into the bed. "I know. I'm a big whale."

"You're the most beautiful woman I have ever seen." Instantly, the tears escaped my closed eyes. I felt miserable. Sure, I was ready to give birth but that wasn't what had me down. It amazed me how Devon had manipulated my heart so bad that it couldn't reciprocate the love that Pete gave me. Silence filled the air as I cried. Pete kissed my tears away and whispered, "You're going to be okay. I got you."

"I know...I know." I fell asleep in his arms and like all other times, I felt safe. I slept for what seemed like forever. I woke up to the smell of fried sausage, pancakes, and eggs and soft jazz music playing. It sounded like Pete was on the phone conversing with one of his drivers. Working my way around him, I made my plate as he talked. Once he hung up the phone, he made himself a plate, he came over and kissed my forehead before sitting down at my two-seater table set with me.

"Damn. You weren't going to wait for me?"

"I'm sorry babe. It smelled so good."

"I see. Your dirty ass ain't wash your face or brush your teeth or nothing. Just wake up and go to the kitchen. Straight savage." Though it hurt to laugh, I could not help but to.

"Stop! You know I have old people's bladder now. If I laugh too hard, I'm going to pee a little." We both laughed our hearts out. It felt good to see him smile. "Thank you for breakfast. It's a new year. What's your goals for the big 2016?"

"To be stable and happy. Insha'Allah, I'll get another truck and some new contracts so I can make more money than I did last year. Save a couple more dollars. And continue to take care of you and the kids. I want you to study estate planning. That way you can set up my estate. So, in the event anything ever happens to me, you and the kids will be straight."

"Pete, you are probably one of Allah's favorite people. You will live a longggg time."

"Probably, but seriously beautiful." I put my head down as a tear escaped my eyelids. "What's wrong?"

"Pete you deserve to be happy and I know I can't make you happy like you deserve to be. I have prayed for the ability to love you like you love me for a long time. I mean I'm great at assisting you with your business. I'm great at helping with Sharif. I'm even good at playing house. But I'm talking about your heart. I feel like I'm incapable of taking care of your heart."

"Shhhhh!"

"No, please. Let me say this. I don't deserve the love you continuously show me, but I need you to know that I appreciate it. Nothing you do or have done for me goes unnoticed. When I just came home, I was penniless and hopeless. I had no idea where I was going to live let alone, how I was going to make enough money to support myself. Per usual, you swooped in and saved me. Any woman would be lucky to have your love, yet you give it to me. Continuously, my heart protects me from you. Or so I thought. Maybe it's protecting you from me." The tears started to pour out. "I miss Malik sooo bad Pete. This pregnancy has made me realize just how much. It has also made me realize that while I have grown in some areas, there are other areas that are still in need of healing. I'm jealous and bitter that you were able to continue on with life without giving it a second thought. You even went on and had another child a year later. Another son at that. And please don't be confused. I love your sons from the bottom of my heart, and you know that. I'll always take care of them and protect them like my own. But for me, that doesn't change that they're a reminder that Malik is gone and never coming back. That's unbearable sometimes. That may be wrong, but I can't help the feelings and it makes me so angry with you and it hinders me from loving you like I should." I put my hands on my face. Pete came closer to me and grabbed my hands.

"Get up." I wiggled from my seat as he helped me to stand. He grabbed my face and kissed my forehead. "I love you Diamond Lewis. Nothing can change that. Even when I want it to change. Do not feel like you have to be stuck or stagnant because of what I do for you. If you find someone that you decide to pursue, just make sure he can do what I do for you or better. And I don't just mean financially. He gotta take care of your heart or he gotta go. No exceptions."

"I didn't say what I said because I'm ready to be with anyone or even date anyone again. I told when we found out that I was pregnant that I was done with dating, so I could focus on baby girl. I was saying that so that you don't feel the need to be a slave to your feelings for me. I want you to be happy. So, if you find someone who makes you happy, don't deny them of your love because of me."

"D, no matter what or who, it's going to be always me & you." Before I could respond, his phone rang, and it was his driver calling back. So, he signaled for me to give him a minute. I drug my ass to the bathroom so that I could get in the shower and get back in bed. While in the shower, I let the hot water run all over my body as I reflected on our conversation. I wondered if I conveyed my message effectively. I wondered if there were other things that kept me from loving him like I should have been, and it always came back to Malik. No matter how many times I said I forgave Pete, it's always that small part of me that wonders if he could have done more to save our baby. I wish GOD would have given me a sign so that my heart could fully forgive him. Pete knocked on the bathroom door breaking my thoughts.

"Come in."

"Hold on Ray. You need help baby?" He asked holding the phone away from his ear. I peeped behind the curtain and nodded with a sad face. Pete placed his phone on speaker as he began washing me. "Go ahead Ahk. I'm listening."

"Well, as I was telling you Ahki. Things aren't looking good. I don't know what to do honestly. I don't want to bring the load back to have to bring it all the way back up here. I gave you the corporate number that's on the form. I'm still here but the guys at the gate aren't budging."

"Yeah. They ain't answering the phone either. I'm about to just shoot up there. I don't see any other options. It's going to take me a minute. If you want, you can grab a room at a hotel where you can park the truck on their parking lot too and I'll reimburse you for the cost. We'll handle delivering the load in the morning and then head back down. Don't worry. You'll be paid a stipend for the idle hours as well."

"Good looking Ahki."

"No problem brother. Thanks for dealing with this bullshit professionally. It is the least I could do. I'll reassign your Texas load, so you can at least get a few days to rest and be with Brittany and the kids."

"Nahhh. I'm good. If we get out of here tomorrow. I'll be good. I'll still have a day home. Then back to the road. I'm on a money mission for this year."

"Already. You know I respect the chase. I'll hit you when I'm close to see where you landed." He concluded his call as he helped me out of the shower. Once we got in the room. He dried me off completely and oiled my entire body. After he helped me put on my bra, panties, and tank top, he attempted to hand me some lounge shorts.

"No sir. Get me some pants and a shirt. Oh, and some crew style socks."

"Where are you going?"

"With you."

"Babe, you can't ride that long. I'm going all the way to Boston."

"I'm going with you."

"I don't think that's a good idea. The doctor said no traveling."

"I'm not due for another week and I'm not even dilating. The doctor said no traveling like planes, boats, trains, etc. He never said I couldn't ride in a car."

"I take it that you are not going to let up. Are you?"

"Nope. So, hand me my shit." I responded as I started doing the cabbage patch dance. We both burst out into laughter. That was the one thing we do that most of; laughed. We literally tripped over everything. He helped me get dressed and get to the car. We agreed that I would not get on his nerves talking his head off the entire time and in exchange, he would stop at the different exits to satisfy my cravings. I was content. I put my earphones on and texted Porsha. I had not seen her face since Christmas Day. She had been on my mind all day though.

    Me: Hey bitch! Why haven't I seen your ugly ass since Christmas?

    Porsha: Not really in a good space. The nigga is packing his shit and leaving me. I was going to tell your childish ass that earlier but you wanted to play on the phone.

    Me: Wow! Why? Were y'all arguing or something? What are your feelings about it?

    Porsha: He done found him a little temporary bitch for real but his ugly ass talking about he can't do this anymore because we're fussing too much, and he needs peace. As bad as I don't want him to leave, I'm not begging the nigga to stay. Nope. Maybe I can really detox from his ass this time for good.

    Me: How you know a female involved? I have never heard you speak of you thinking he was cheating before.

Porsha: Bitch because I know my nigga. It's a lot of shit that I don't speak on that happens in this household because I can hold my own. You know that.

Me: Damn. So, this just came out of nowhere?

Porsha: No, him leaving ain't come out of nowhere. He been planning this shit but never said anything. Lately, we've just been fussing and fighting consistently about any and everything. So, I told myself I wasn't arguing with his ass anymore because I refuse to expose McKenzie to the toxic shit.

Me: Wow! I really can't believe this is happening for real.

Porsha: Me either. I gave this nigga twelve years, a kid, and two bids. Took care of my daughter on my own in his absence and this is the thanks I get. If I didn't have McKenzie, I'd risk it all and take it all the way there with him.

Me: There's always more than one way to skin a cat. I'm going up Boston with Pete. We'll be back tonight. Let McKenzie be your strength until I get there. Don't let her see you break. Cry in the bathroom or even sit in your car. Do not break down in front of her. I love you SG.

Porsha: Bet. I love you too SG.

Me: Forever.

Porsha: Forever.

Pete looked over at me but said nothing. We cruised and listened to tunes. He even let me listen to my sad love songs. We had made it all the way to Philadelphia before I requested that we stop and that's only because I had to urinate. Pete had asked me as we approached different exits if I wanted to try this food or that food. Honestly, my appetite was gone completely. Porsha was on my mind so heavy. We'd been close our entire lives; almost as if we were connected like twins. So, when she hurt, I hurt. Right now, my heart was completely broken. Porsha was the epitome of loyal. On the many of accounts that I knew of that she could've left Ty, she never did. She was completely committed to her family and she rode hard for them.

"Come on beautiful." I looked around. I was so deep in thought that I hadn't noticed that we'd pulled into the rest stop and Pete had opened the door for me.

"My bad babe." I said as he helped me out of the car.

"Remember what I told you! That nigga gotta treat you better than me or his ass gotta go. If you choose less, just make sure it isn't going to affect my daughter."

"Huh?" I responded confusedly. He looked at my phone. "Oh noooo! You shouldn't assume. You're terribly wrong." I giggled. "I am not seeing anyone Pete. You'd be the first person I tell. I promise you that. Jealously looks a little sexy on you though."

"Thank you! I respect that." he responded as he nodded.

"Of course. But one thing. Promise me that you won't wait until I find someone for you to move on. Don't burden yourself with that responsibility."

"I Promise!" He said staring directly in my eyes.

Chapter Nine

We stayed overnight in Boston and Pete had left this morning to handle his business with work. I slept for most of the day because I was in pain, but I refused to admit that to Pete. He would have started fussing about how I should have stayed home and all that. Truth be told, now I wish I did. Not only was I uncomfortable but I was worried about Porsha. We had talked briefly but I did not want Pete knowing what was going on with her business, so I cut the conversation short. I did not want to risk him coming in while I was talking. He knew how I was about my siblings, especially Porsha, so he would be worried and even more overprotective and overcrowding my space. Just as I was about to text Porsha, Pete came in.

"Get ready Beautiful. It's time for us to leave"

"I'm ready babe. Just give me a second to use the bathroom before we get on the road."

"Need some help?" He offered.

"No. I got it." I locked to the door to the bathroom behind and exhale heavily. Pete phone rung and he answered but asked the caller to allow him to call them right back. He knocked at the door of the bathroom.

"You good D?"

"Yes, I'm fine. Be out in a minute."

"Take your time. I'm about to step out and make a call."

"Okay." I responded as I figured he was leaving out to talk privately about something for his business. He'd been doing that lately, so I didn't think deep into it. I finished using the bathroom and fixed my hair in the mirror. When I entered the room again, Pete still wasn't in the room. I put on my coat, hat, and scarf. I opened the door to find him leaning on the wall, back facing me on the phone. Usually he was on point, but Pete was deeply indulged in his conversation. I stood there silently and listened.

"Baby, I told you I'm in Boston. I have to make a stop in New York to holla at my Pops then I'm coming straight home to y'all...You're right. I should've called...You know if it wasn't work, I would've been there. Come on now...You got that. I apologize. It won't happen again...What are you cooking?...Damn! Oh yeah. I'll coming straight in the house when I get in town so text me if you need anything before I get home...Where is Sharif?... Oh okay. Go ahead beautiful. I love you more. Kiss my prince for me." He concluded his call with Nita, Sharif's mother. Home was the only word that kept repeating itself in my head. I know I told him to move on and be happy. Seemed to me though like he was already doing that which was not an issue. A few things were bothering me though. Mainly how he was consistently pressing down on me about if I was seeing someone. I see now that was only to justify his own actions. After ending his call, he placed his phone in his pocket and turned to walk back into the room only to find me staring at him.

"D..." He started to say something, but I put my hand up to stop him.

"I'll be in the lobby." I said and walked pass him before he could see my tears fall. I pressed the button for the elevator to go down. Once the elevator doors closed behind me, I screamed so loud. It was then that I realized that no matter what I tried to tell myself or anyone else different, against my will, I had fallen for Pete. It was too late though. My pride had pushed him back to Nita. As the doors opened, I quickly got myself together. I grabbed a few napkins from the front desk and plopped down in one of the lobby's large lobby chairs. It made sense though. We hadn't had sex since I was seven months. Pete usually wanted to have sex every day and if were up to me, it would be multiple times a day but lately, his excuses were consistent, and our sex life was absent. Well, mine anyway. I pulled out my phone and group texted Porsha & Lilly.

    Me: I hate niggas. I'm boutta find me a bitch again.

    Porsha: Absolutely not bitch. What's going on?

    Lilly: D, you gotta find the strength to bury those feelings for Devon's no good behind.

    Porsha: Shut the fuck up Lil. How you know this got anything to do with Devon?

    Porsha: Hellooooo? Earth to fucking Diamond.

    Porsha: Bitch, please don't tell me it's Devon.

I struggled with whether I wanted to expose my feelings or not.

    Me: Hell no. I ain't fucking with nobody's broke ass inmate.

    Lilly: Okay so I am lost.

    Porsha: Me too so D enlighten us bitch!

    Me: Pete.

    Lilly: OMG! What could Pete have done?

    Porsha: I will beat the shit out of Peter. What the fuck happened?

    Me: He is back with Nita.

    Porsha: Bitch, you are lyingggggg!

Me: I overheard him talking to her in the hallway of our hotel room.

Lilly: Maybe he is decided to get back with her opposed to meeting someone new. That would not be wrong. You know Pete is a family man for real. Besides, you do not want him in that way and I'm sure that's not going to stop him from taking care of you so what's the issue?

Me: That is not the point. Nevermind.

Porsha: Shut your whiny ass up bitch. You just think she is going to cut into them coins. Besides, you could have heard it wrong.

Me: Porsha, I know what I heard. Besides, I could see it in his eyes.

Lilly: Oh Lord! You got caught eavesdropping?

Me: I did not necessarily hide. I was getting ready to meet him so we could leave. When I left the room, he was in the hallway on the phone, so I stood there and listened. The nigga was so off point I could have tagged him if I was an opp.

Porsha: Okay, this is unusual, but I agree with Lilly to a certain degree. Couple things are off though. First and foremost, why the fuck is he still playing house with you if he decided to be back with her? As a man, he should have kept it funky with you. I do not respect that. Secondly, you are too grown to be playing games. If you are feeling the nigga, then you should have either fell back or let him know. So, that is on you too bitch.

Lilly: Porsha, really? No matter what your feelings are, I'm here as a sounding board D.

I did not respond. I raised my head to Pete looking at me and I rolled my eyes. Pete attempted to help me while I was getting up, but I snatched my arm away from him. He walked ahead of me to the car and opened my door. I got in, put my earphones in, and turned my music up. I bumped my head song after song, and it was distracting me from those floating feelings that I could not place. I did not want to say anything to Pete, so I was relieved when he pulled into a rest stop. I had been holding my urine for about 15 minutes and it was starting to hurt my stomach. I felt like I released 10 pounds after I urinated. I went to the restaurant attached to the rest stop so that I could grab a bite to eat primarily to feed my baby because I had no appetite. After settling back in the car, I put my earphones back in my ear, reclined my chair, and dozed off. We pulled into the parking lot of Rikers Island. I woke up to Pete shaking me gently and removing my ear plug.

"Come on D."

"I'm not going in there. Tell Big Pete I said hi."

"You can't sit in here that long. It's fucking freezing out here."

"I'm not going anywhere with you. Therefore, I'm not going the fuck in. Don't miss your visit sitting here arguing with me because I'm not changing my mind." I put my earphone back in and dozed right back off. I slept like a baby until Pete opened the car door to get in. The cold air caused me to shiver. I don't even know how long I slept but I felt rejuvenated.

"Are you okay?" Pete asked.

"I gotta pee." I responded as I rolled my eyes.

"D, let's just talk about it and get whatever you're feeling out there."

"You don't owe me an explanation and I don't you any conversation. Take me to a restroom please."

"We gotta..."

"I ain't gotta do shit but piss and if you don't want me to piss on this chair, I suggest you start this fucking car and find me a restroom." The tears started to flow again. I hated so badly that I could not control my emotions. I was so upset that I was hyperventilating.

"Baby, talk to me please so you can calm down. You can hurt the baby stressing. Talk to me!"

"No, Pete. There is nothing to talk about. Please. Just pull off. I really want to go home." He started the car and I wiggled as I sat up in my chair. I was instantly irritated when I realized that my phone had went dead while I was sleep. I bent over to put my phone on the charger and a sharp pain shot up my side. I screamed.

"Are you okay?" Pete asked.

"No! I'm having contractions." I was surprised because I hadn't had any this painful throughout my entire pregnancy. I gasped for air as I screamed from the surprise of the next contraction which came about 10 minutes later and lasted for what felt like forever. "Shit! Shit! Shit!" Pete said as he swiftly maneuvered through traffic.

"Hospitallll!" I cried through my next contraction. I was breathing rapidly. I closed my eyes and I sat my chair back some. Just as Pete was pulling into Harlem Hospital Center, my contractions were coming more frequently and lasting longer. Pete pulled in front of the Emergency Room, hopped out, and ran inside shouting.

The nurses came rushing out behind Pete with a gurney and assisted me with getting on it. Another contraction occurred just as my water broke and I screamed out from the severe pain. Pete rubbed my head as I was brawling.

"It's okay baby! Just breathe." It sounded as if he was on the brink of crying himself. I knew how special this was for him. He had not seen Malik born because Devon was there with me and made me put Pete on the Do Not Admit list. Unfortunately, he was not able to see Tyrik or Sharif born because Nita was mad at him about me both times. My sympathy tripled for him in that moment as I realized I robbed him of all of those moments. Though I was not happy to be having my baby hundreds of miles away from home, I was happy that he could have this experience. My next contraction felt like it wanted to take me out.

"Aaaaaahhhhhhh!" I screamed.

"Aren't y'all gonna give her an epidural? Y'all see she's in pain." Pete said as we entered the emergency delivery room.

"I promise you sir. Your wife is going to be fine."

"SHE'S NOT FINE NOW! GET HER SOMETHING!" He yelled. They rushed to begin removing my clothes. "Man, cut that shit off or something man. My baby hurting man. Come on now. Y'all killing me."

"Sir you have to step back and let us do our job! I promise you we are going to take care of her." By the time she finished her sentence, I was undressed and pushing. The doctor advised against giving me an epidural because of how rapidly I was dilating and experiencing contractions. I cried, screamed, and pushed for what felt like forever, but was really only 15 minutes. Baby girl was almost out but I felt too weak to push again.

"Diamond, you have to push sweetie or little girl is going to lose oxygen." The nurse informed me. I was tired and out of breath, but I gave one last push with everything I had in me. Just like that, the entire world was blessed with my baby girl. She was seven pounds and seven ounces with a beautiful round face and dimples just like Pete's mother, Ms. Sonya. Pete kissed my face what seemed like a thousand times. We had discussed thousands of names and though we'd decided and agreed on one, I didn't use it. I named her Harlym Sonya Newman. I knew how much Pete missed his mom and now he'd be able to have a piece of her and feel close to her again. Immediately after being cleaned up, I was given pain meds and I was out like a light. When I woke up, I heard lots of laughter. I opened my eyes and saw my room full of family. Porsha, Lee, Aunt Babs, Rell, and my mother were all sitting around, laughing and joking. I looked around for my baby girl and saw that she was right next to me sleeping peacefully in the bedside crib.

"Damn. How long was I out?" I said in a low tone as I tried to sit up. I felt numb a bit.

"Bitch, my niece is a fucking BOMB! Boom! I cannot wait to dress her up and do her hair every fucking day!" Porsha said excitedly.

"Why do you always curse so much? Your mouth is filthy!" My mother said to Porsha.

"Kat don't fuck-ing start with me. Okay?" Porsha said with her neck rolling.

"Little girl..." Kat started.

"Oh nope. I'm not having any of that around my daughter so if y'all can't chill out for the sake of her, y'all can leave now!" I said to everyone. The room fell quiet for a moment.

"Bitch fuck you. It's a party in this bitch!" Lee said as he started to dance and slapped my foot.

"Ouch bitch that hurts." I laughed. "Your dumb ass." Everyone joined in dancing with him and I felt so happy, loved, and supported. My family had really been showing up for me. I knew GOD was responsible. Thank you, GOD. Rell & Lee went to get me some food. Porsha and Aunt Babz went to get me and baby girl some clothes. Porsha loved any excuse to shop but I was grateful for her. That left Harlym, Kat, and myself which meant the room was very quiet. I picked my daughter up and held her close to me. I was so happy. She was perfect in every way; perfectly beautiful and perfectly healthy. I closed my eyes as I smelled her and thanked GOD again for not making my baby suffer as a result of my pour choice of drinking with her. I rocked her and sung to her. I was just laying her down from breast feeding her when someone knocked at the door. It was a delivery man.

"Hello. Are you Ms. Diamond Lewis?" He asked me.

"Why? Who wants to know?" Kat jumped up.

"I have a floral arrangement delivery for Ms. Lewis. Am I at the wrong room?" He asked looking back and forth at the door number and his clipboard.

"No sir. You are at the right room. Don't mind this nut. Sit down somewhere." I said and giggled at Kat. Much like Porsha, she was always ready to battle.

"Okay, good. I would hate to have to take these beautiful flowers back." The delivery man wheeled in the 7 dozen of fresh daisies. I inhaled the daises and knew that Pete had sent them as they all smelled like Marc Jacobs Daisy. Kat brought me the card that the delivery man handed her after she signed for the flowers.

Thank you for my greatest gift to date. You are officially the strongest woman I know. I love you Beautiful. Pete.

I smiled for all of five seconds before my mind traveled to back to his conversation in the hallway. The word home played over again until my ears rung.

"Are you okay baby girl?" Kat asked.

"Yes ma'am. I'm fine. Just lost in my thoughts. Thanks for coming."

"It was my pleasure. Thank you for allowing me to stay once you got up with your stubborn behind." I smiled as Kat kissed my forehead. "You did so great I heard without any meds. I could not imagine. You and Pete made me the most beautiful glam baby ever." I thought back to the events of yesterday. Pete deserved to be happy and if I was not sure of anything else, I knew Nita really loved and appreciated him. I also knew that their relationship would not affect his ability to help me raise and take care of Harlym. He was always by my side when it mattered the most. At least that is what my mind reasoned. My heart had officially shut down to the idea of him.

"When is Pete coming back?" I asked with a wide smile. His absence made me assume he may be using the time we were in New York to visit his father's family.

"I'm not sure he is baby. He left instructions with Porsha & Lee. He had to get back to Baltimore. Something was going on with Sharif I believe."

"Wow." I said aloud as my smile faded. There was not a damn thing wrong with Sharif. Pete really left me and my daughter so that he could make it home to Nita. "Do me a favor please and throw all of those flowers in the trash." I said to Kat.

"Are you sure?" She asked, confused at my request.

"Positive!"

"Can I keep one for myself if you don't want them?"

"THROW THEM IN THE TRASH!" I screamed.

Kat rambled out loud about slapping the shit out of one of us one day as she threw the flowers in the hospital room's trashcan. I didn't mean to yell at her as I knew that she suffered from a series of mental health issues. She continued on and on, but I was lost in my own thoughts. Pete had just earned his way on my shit list.

Chapter Ten

The first step towards going somewhere is deciding that you are not going to stay where you are. Do I really need to get into details about how I cussed Pete ass out when I made it back to Maryland? Yeah, well I did that and some; like bust the living room window of his house and the windshield of his truck. I would have done more than that, but he was so mad he threatened to shoot me. Chileee! That man had murder in his eyes, so I decided to just leave. I kept on my poker face, but I was nervous as a mother fucker.

That had been eighteen months ago and so much had changed in that time. The first change was that I moved from the studio Pete had gotten me in Columbia into my own two-bedroom apartment in West Baltimore. It was not what I had gotten used to but I damn sure was not one to act like I was too good for standard. It was clean, renovated, and big enough for me and Harlym. I missed my studio every day and though I acted on my feelings, I felt it was necessary to move forward.

Of course, I laced my apartment just like any other place I have had but one thing I had to learn was how to budget and pay bills. That was no easy plight; especially since Pete had cut me off financially. So, once I completed drug court, I picked up a second job. That was short lived because after about 6 months, I felt like I had missed some essential moments with Harlym. Like hearing her first words and being there for her first step. So, I left that job. It was not like I needed a lot of extra money. All I did was work and stay in the house with Harlym. Pete did everything for Harlym so I never had to worry about her needs not being met. My stash was depleting, and I had to think of an idea fast to get some money or I was going to be making life decisions between paying my phone bill or getting an oil change. One day I bumped into Trina. She had graduated the program, was working, and needed a place for her and her son. We sat down, talked about it, and decided to be roommates. I drew up a contract that required us to split all the house bills. She agreed and signed, and that was a huge relief for me. It still was not enough though. After I paid my half of the bills, paid my car insurance, bought groceries & household items, and bought gas, I was literally only able to add $300 to my stash every two weeks. But with me having to make ends meet, I was even dipping in my stash here and there too.

It was one week until Christmas and two weeks before Harlym's first birthday and I was down to my last. I had vowed not to touch my stash and I felt defeated. I was not hopeless though. I had Porsha to reach out to Charisma. He met with us the next evening to negotiate pay. Well, his intentions were to tell us what he was going to pay us. I was not having that though. He knew we were thorough and solid. I need to be able to take care of my daughter, put up in my stash, invest in my own estate, and pay my lawyer a retainer. He agreed to my price and just like that, we were back in the game. You can tell he did not really have any reliable people. My first three runs were in the same week. I felt like shit throwing bricks at the penitentiary but the joy I felt to be able to provide for my baby girl balanced it out for me. I threw Harlym the biggest first birthday party ever and guess what? She was not even impressed. Pete had bought her a Minnie Mouse Jeep and she was in love. She did not want to eat, play, dance, or open any other gifts. I was jealous. Here I went out of my way to give her the biggest Minnie Mouse bash ever and all she wanted was that damn jeep. My feelings were hurt, and I did not want Pete to there anymore, but I'd never deny him of anything involving Harlym. Besides, she would not let me. Their bond was inseparable.

    Of course, Pete had a million questions about where I got the money to throw such an extravagant party and every single one of those questions went unanswered. However, unwilling to ruin his daughter's special day, he just let it go. In fact, after that day, he let everything go when it came to me. He used to pay my electric bill every so often and pay my rent at the rental office sometimes but not after that birthday party. I was okay with it though. The less help I had, the harder I went. Oh, and the money I was making with Charisma was plentiful. That $300 I was adding to the stash every two weeks quickly turned into $1000 a week. I ain't plan on hustling for a long time. In fact, I had six months left because I had six months left until Harlym's second birthday and I was out. After that, I was buying a house up in Jersey with my family.

I kept my job at the center for security and I only made runs on Wednesday evenings. This Wednesday was not any different. Damn! I thought as I sucked air through the straw of what had a few minutes ago been my Dunkin Donuts Iced Coffee. I still had 40 minutes to drive before I reached my destination in Philly, so I was glad that I got two expresso shots. They had yet to kick in, and my body felt so drained. I turned the air on and adjusted the radio to play the music from my phone.

Last tear just fell from my eyes

Told myself that I wasn't going to cry no more

(you did what you did, it is what it is)

And that's why I walked out the door

Moved on with my life, but not really

Spent too much time wondering how could you

(you do this to us while we we're in love)

I guess I was thinking too much

I bounced and danced as I sang my heart out with Auntie Mo and my thoughts shifted right to Pete. Tears began to flow uncontrollably as I thought back on the good times that we had and how close we used to be. It seemed like I was on a consistent emotional roller coaster without him. Sure, I had dated since leaving Pete. I had not met anyone that I had made it to a second date with; let alone be interested enough to take them seriously. That did not stop me from believing love could happen for me though. Love had happened for Pete and though we were not on good terms right now, I was happy for him. No man I knew deserved love more than Pete. It was not just that easy though because I had finally admitted to myself that I would have rather been the one making him happy. Don't know what you have until it's gone, right? I know and to make matters worse, a few months ago, he married Nita.

It was the most beautiful wedding ever. No, I did not go but I allowed Harlym to be a part of their wedding. A couple weeks later Nita granted me access to her wedding photo album online claiming that was so that I could get the pictures of Harlym. I knew that was a lie because she could have just emailed me the pictures of Harlym. She just wanted me to see her big beautiful wedding as an attempt to make me jealous. I was not jealous though because I knew that Pete's ideal wedding was a small traditional Muslim service called Nikah at the Masjid. He had always talked about it.

An entire playlist of songs later, I pulled up to the car garage and got out to tap on the valet box window. A mexican guy came out from the back.

"Let me get this ticket for you darling."

"Nahhh. I'm good. Where's Bahar?"

"He's out to Lunch. I'll park it for you." I panicked internally a little because that wasn't a part of the routine. Bahar knew his big greasy ass should've been here. I had to think quick. "Nahhhh. I'm good. Last time I let someone else other than Bahar park my car, y'all got a scratch on my shit." I pointed to a scratch that Harlym had put on my car with her jeep. "I'll wait in my car for him. Thank you." Just as I was getting in my car, Bahar came walking swiftly into the entrance of the garage.

"Hello Friend!"

"Hello shit! Be on time at all times. I got shit to do."

"My apologies my friend."

I left the garage and walked to Terminal Market to grab a bite to eat to allow the allotted hour to pass. I made sure to grab Harlym some cake from the sweets stand and grab Trina's black soap that she likes. I sat down to eat and messaged Pete to check on Harlym.

Me: Hey. What's my baby doing?

Pete: Nothing much. We are outside around the way. Chilling. Do you want her to talk to her?

Me: If that's cool.

I fixed my hair in my camera and applied some lipstick. Just as I was doing my final check, Pete was calling me on FaceTime.. Pete appeared on the phone holding Harlym. Quickly, I realized that he was studying my background and moved the phone closer to my face.

"You are pretty good!" He stated but I did not respond.

"Mommyyyyyy!" Harlym screamed excitedly.

"Hey Mommy's baby! Mommy miss you! Are you having fun with Daddy?"

"Yessss!"

"Awww! But Mommy's ready for you to come home Tinka Momma?"

"What time you want me to bring her home?" Pete asked.

"I'll be home like 8 or 9"

"That's late Diamond. Let me just keep her."

"No!" I shouted with an attitude. He already knew how I felt about my daughter staying away from me overnight. Knowing he did not mean any harm; I calmed my voice and tone. "Come on now. Don't do that Pete."

"Don't do what? Travel with my daughter at 9 o'clock at night to West Baltimore City?"

"Pete, you know I'm working so I can talk care of my daughter."

"Working? That's what you call it? Working? You're so addicted to a lifestyle – a fairy tale lifestyle - that could very well take you away from your daughter. You and I both know that the shit never ends well." I was taken by surprise at how much it appeared he knew.

"What are you talking about?" I knew I was caught but I kept a straight face. "Besides, it ended well for you right?"

"Mannn, talk to your daughter before you make me mad." He shifted the phone to Harlym.

"Hey Baby Girl! Mommy will see you very soon baby."

"Mommyyyyyy!" Harlym screamed again and smiled. Her smile warmed my heart.

"I love you Tinky!"

"I wuv you! Bye Bye Mommy!"

The phone disconnected before I could say anything else. Pete had some fucking nerve. He really got under my skin sometimes. Mainly, when he was right though. This is a lifestyle I needed to take care of my daughter how I wanted to. I was smart. I had already enrolled to go back to school. I would be making great money once I finished since I had experience from doing Lilly's books from her businesses. That just seemed so long away though. I still did not like Pete calling himself putting me in my place.

Me: Don't ever fucking hang up on me while I'm talking to my fucking daughter.

Pete: Fuck you.

Me: Fuck you Clown!

I was so pissed off in that moment, that I had to laugh. He had gotten so good at being tough with me. Far from the sucker for love he used to be. I hated it but my heart softened because he was right. Little did he know that made me more attracted to him.

"Six more months and I am done." I said out loud and checked my watch. I had 15 minutes left before I had to pick the car up, so I just utilized that time to eat and think. Ding! Ding! Ding! My alarm went off and I cleaned off the table where I had eaten and made my way back to the garage. I picked up the car with no issues or delays and, after stopping at Dunkin Donuts to reup on coffee, I was on my way back to Baltimore. I was severely tired and tried to avoid falling asleep several times. I shook my head and opened my eyes wide to shake the sleep off. That did not work but my phone rung. It was Lee. I figured that was perfect. I would get him to talk to me until I got back.

"Sisssss!" Lee yelled as soon as I answered his call.

"You are always right on time."

"What's up Baby Girl?"

"Where should I start?"

"The beginning is always best."

We talked, laughed, and sang songs until my heart was full. I was so happy to have some real love still left around me. Lee put some things in perspective for me. I was not in love with Devon. I was in love with what he provided for me. Once that stopped so did my feelings for him. He explained how it went back to our family roots.

My mother was a paper chaser; always well taken care of by the expense of whoever her man was at the time. All my sisters, even though they are educated and in good careers, are still taken care of by the earnings of their men. Even my grandfather took care of my grandmother and now Mr. Kevin. Aunt Babz was a hustler since before I was born. Grandma Mae, my mother, or Aunt Babz never worked a day in their lives. It all made sense. Then to top it off, I had inherited abandonment issues from both my mother and father. So, on top of loving being taken care of, I hated being alone.

Therefore, I allowed certain things to occur or I settled for less than I was worth for the sake of being with someone and being taken care of. It was crystal clear, and I was happy that someone made sense of it for me. I had to change the narrative. Not just for me, but for Harlym. I wanted her to see what healthy love looked like so that she would learn how to love for the right reasons. You know. The way Pete used to love me. I noticed that I had been sitting parked five minutes which I never did because someone always raised the garage at one minute exactly. Just as I reached for my phone, the garage door raised. I hesitated and looked around before proceeding to back my car into the garage. Again, I had that eerie feeling of being watched but I proceeded, completed the drop off, picked my baby up, and made it in safe.

"Six more months." I said aloud after I shut my house door. "Just six more months."

Chapter Eleven

It had been six months since I promised myself that I was out in six months. That could not have been further from the truth. I switched my runs from Wednesdays to Saturdays and even picked up a different run on Sundays. I was addicted; so much so that I eventually gave in and allowed Pete to keep Harlym on the weekends. While he was ecstatic to have her every weekend, you can tell he worried about what my itinerary entailed. No matter how mad he was at me about anything, his love always projected louder than his anger.

It was a Friday night and I had just dropped her off. Christmas was Monday so not only did I have my runs, but I also had to Christmas shop as well. Let us not fail to mention that I had her birthday to plan. But first, I was going to get me something to eat. As I rode down Monument Street, my mouth watered at the thought of some chicken from Panda's, so I made it my business to stop. It was late so there were few patrons in the store which was even better. As I entered, a gentleman who was standing in the back corner near the store's entrance opened the door for me.

"Thanks, handsome." I said without giving him a good look over, but he smelled amazing.

"You're welcome sexy." I giggled. I was not a fan of being called sexy, but I loved to be complimented when I was dressed down. I flashed a smile to display my gratitude. I walked up to the counter and ordered me a chicken box and a Panda Punch. I made sure to tuck my change before I turned around. Let me tell you something though. When I did turn around, Mr. Handsome was standing there leaning against the store's glass window looking good as a mother fucker. He was wearing a 7 For All Mankind jean set, a grey and white pullover Hugo Boss hoodie underneath his jacket, a grey Louis Vuitton belt, and grey 990s on his feet. Oddly, he had black store bag tied on his front belt loop. He was a drug dealer; I suspected. My suspicious were confirmed almost immediately. A white couple came in and the man handed him some money.

"Wait in front of Save – A – Lot." He instructed them. As they left out, he counted the money, separated some into two handful, and tucked both handfuls in different pockets. Then, he proceeded to untie the black bag, count out 4 baggies, and retie the bag while holding those that he counted out in his hand.

"Ma'am, your food ready." The Chinese man called out to me. I turned around to get my food and lemonade as well as check it to make sure it was correct. Once I was satisfied, I turned to leave out. I noticed that though Mr. Handsome was gone, he had dropped some money where he was standing.

Against my better judgement, I picked the money up, $160, and left the store. I sat my food and beverage in my car before tucking my nine in my back behind me. Pete made me become a license gun owner as well as get a permit to carry now that Harlym and I lived so far away from him. It was solemnly for our protection, not for nights like these when I decided to make crazy decisions like tonight. Better safe than sorry. Though I knew the best form of safety would have been minding my business. I proceeded to walk across the street to Save – A – Lot. As I approached, I noticed him standing there, frustrated with something on his phone. "I'm not-fussing-with-you-about-any-dumb-shit. Don't-call-my-phone-anymore." He said into the phone. My first thought was that he was being sarcastic to whoever occupied the other line of the phone, but I realized after he finished his statement that he was sending a voice recording.

"Excuse me Mr. Handsome."

"Heyyyy. My girl. Ms. Sexy. What's up baby?" I was relieved that he didn't have a speech problem.

"Did you drop a dollar?" I said holding my hand out to give him the hundred-dollar bill and three twenties. He checked his pockets pulling out money from every pocket and returning it after checking its contents. Finally, he found the pocket where it was missing from. Finally, he took the money from me.

"Damn. Thank you. Thank you. Thank you." He responded genuinely. "Thank you so much love. I really appreciate that. The average female would have taken that and copped themselves some shit.

"Ain't nothing average 'bout me. But you're welcome. Be safe out here."

"Already."

I turned around to walk back to my car. I was praying that my fries weren't soggy. I opened my box if food and ate a few fries before deciding that I wanted to eat at a table. So, I decided to make my way to Aunt Babs house since it was the closest. My phone rung and it was Porsha calling me on FaceTime..

"Hey Bitchhhhh!" she yelled through the phone.

"Bitch, have you been drinking?" I laughed.

"I absolutely have. I'm down Aunt Babs shit. Come through yo. All of us down here."

"That's crazy. I'm on my way there anyway so I can eat my food."

"Yessss Bitch. Bring me some because I need to feed this liquorrrrr." Porsha responded.

"Oh, hell no. You better send someone to get you some food. That's dead Bitch."

"Bitch, you are selfish."

"Oh, really? I had a tea for you too bitch. I ain't telling you now." I said and licked my tongue out at her.

"Did I tell you that you are looking the fuck good today bitch?"

"Bitch, I am looking plain, bare faced and all. Don't try me hoe." We both laughed at her attempt to get back in my good graces. You know we live for a good pot of tea.

"I'll see you when I get there, fool." About five minutes later, I pulled up to Aunt Babs house to see Lee and Rell sitting out front politicking. The conversation looked intense. I made a mental note to holla at Rell to see what the conversation was about. I grabbed my purse, food, and lemonade and went in the house after showing them some love.

"The realest bitch is hereeeee." I screamed as I entered the living room of Aunt Babs house. "Hey Sisss." Lilly said as we hugged and exchanged cheek kisses.

"You look cute."

"I look regular as shit though."

"I like the bare look on you. It allows your beauty to radiate from the inside." Lilly said as a matter of fact like.

"Awww! Thanks, Lil!" I beamed. I needed some commendation. I had been down lately. I missed Pete like crazy in different ways. I missed the sex as I had not had sex since we parted ways. I missed the companionship; having someone to lay up and cuddle with. Above all, I missed our friendship. No one else had been to me what he was, and I fucked that up because I wanted to be in the mix. Women would kill for a man who wanted to take care of every one of their needs and here I had handed mine to the next woman.

"Don't pump that weak ass bitch up!" Porsha yelled from the kitchen.

"It's always a clown ass bitch on that hating shit. Fuck you hoe." I responded as we hugged for what seemed like forever. Could she feel that I needed a hug? "Thank you, sis!"

"Anytime. Now where is the food?"

"Bitch!" We both laughed and of course, we both ate and drank Lemonade while we spilled tea. After a while, the drink had taken over and she was sleep. In fact, the crowd had died down and everyone was gone; except Porsha who was drunk sleep on the chair next to me. I laid on her leg and decided to get on my phone until I felt like driving to go home. I scrolled through Facebook for some entertainment and stop at the People You May Know section. The first person to pop up was Mr. Handsome. His profile name read Almighty Dollar'Bill. It could not be the same person. I shook Porsha hard as I could. "Get up bitch!"

"What's wrong?" Porsha said as she jumped up.

"Bitch...Bitch...Bitch!"

"What Bitch? My mother fucking head hurts. What the fuck do you want?" Porsha said seriously. I laughed so hard my stomach started hurting. "You are a stupid ass bitch." She said as she burst out into laughter.

"Dead serious though. Why the fuck I think this is the nigga Dollar Bill?"

"Where Bitch?" She asked sitting up at full attention.

"On my phone girl!" I beamed as I tossed her the phone.

"Bitch, let me wake all the way up. Explain to me how he got there and how you know it's that Dollar Bill." Porsha requested so I broke down the store to her about him dropping his money and so forth.

"Oh Wowww." She started. "So, I can tell you are digging the nigga by how your brown skin is glowing red. You know damn well I'm going to rock with whatever decision you make after this conversation but let me keep it funky with you. First thing first, you know what comes with fucking with a nigga that plays the block. You have been there. The only difference is you were a juvenile then. You are an adult now with your own dirt and a baby girl depending on you. For two, the nigga sloppy as fuck with his business for you to be able to run down the entire move he busted. Then he careless with the money. For three, what is our number one rule? No hustlers with social media. You know we do not do niggas that is all in the mix. But like I said, I am with whatever you with. Just do not put us in position to have to do the nigga dirty. 'Cause you know I ain't gonna play bout you, right?"

"Already. But I don't want any relationship or anything like that. I just like his vibe."

"Bitch, you don't know how to not be in a relationship."

"True. Well, we'll see." I responded as I hit the button to send a friend request. Seconds later, Lee bust in Aunt Babs house yelling for Rell. I made a mental note to start making sure that door locked. The last thing I wanted to do was be in here chilling and a nigga have beef with Lee or Rell and run up in here.

"Aye yo. Where Rell?" He asked out of breath.

"Upstairs. What the fuck is wrong with you?" Porsha asked concerned but he didn't answer. He just ran past us up the steps. He ran right back down the steps yelling again.

"Man, he not up there. Where he at yo? I'm not playing. I need his fucking gun!"

"What the fuck is going on?" I asked.

"Mannnn, that shit doesn't matter right now. I need a tone."

"What happened to the last one you had that I got you?" I asked.

"What the fuck you think happened?"

"Oh, that's tough! I don't know what to tell you." As soon as I finished my sentence, you could hear gun shots let off outside. "Oh shit."

"FUCK!" Lee yelled angrily.

"Here yo." I said as I untucked my gun from behind me and handed it to him. "Don't bring that shit here!" I yelled after him as he was running out the door.

"Why you ain't been give him the gun bitch?" Porsha asked me with an attitude.

"Why the fuck you ain't give him yours bitch?" I retorted

"Obviously, I ain't got one on me or it wouldn't have been an issue."

"I guess not. Yours ain't legal bitch. Mine is. Now I gotta go report my gun stolen...AGAIN! You think them people stupid. I get guns to protect me and my daughter. Not to lace Lee with artillery for beef he probably got into about a bitch."

"It doesn't matter what the fuck it is about. Does he question you what it is about when he goes in that water bout you? No, the fuck he does not. He just rides. Do not get so set in your ways, that you forget that your shit stink too. And that someone else has had to wipe it sometimes." Porsha said rolling her eyes.

"Porsha if you don't get the fuck out of my face bitch! That's my mother fucking shit bitch. I'll do what the fuck I please with it." I said pissed off.

"Let me get my shit so I can go before you really take me the fuck there bitch."

"Cut that shit out right now & I mean it!" Aunt Babs said as she came down the steps.

"That's that dusty ass bitch was going to leave my brother on stuck!" Porsha spat.

"Dusty? Bitch, dusty? Do you really want to go there with me hoe?" I said walking towards her.

"I said shut the fuck up and I mean right mother fucking now or I will slap the shit out of both of you bitches." Aunt Babs said and the room fell silent. "D, that was fucked up. You know that. But Porsha, that girl has been having y'all mother fucking backs her entire fucking life. Goddamn! Y'all act like it's a mother fucking problem when that girl says no. She has the right to say no! Who the fuck do y'all think y'all are?" Aunt Babs asked.

"I'm not asking anybody to carry me. I hold my own but better believe if I can be there for any of my blood, I do." Porsha said.

"How am I not being there for y'all because I don't want to give my registered gun to my brother for his street beef?"

"What? That's what this is about?" Aunt Babs looked at Porsha sternly. "For you to be so educated, you love to live this ghetto hoodrat lifestyle Tyrone has gotten you accustomed to! That's not how you were raised."

"I'm not a fucking hoodrat!"

"Bitch you are whatever the fuck I call you in my shit! Porsha, it is time to grow the fuck up. Nobody deserves to spend their entire life saving you stupid mother fuckers. How many times has that girl saved Lee's ass this year alone? Let's see." She said as started counting on her fingers. "She paid Bird for the packs he stole in the spring so he wouldn't kill his ass. She paid his damn rent twice over the summer so he would not be homeless even though he got that no good ass bitch laying up in there with her dusty ass. She gave him and Rell her first two guns, even against her better judgement and even risked beefing with Pete about it. Not to mention all that she does for the rest of y'all. Give her a fucking break." The tears started to flow down my face. It felt like a weight had been pulled off my shoulders. She turned to me and continued. "You do not have to be held bound by the responsibility of your siblings. These are your mother's children. They are no longer your responsibility. Free yourself, find yourself, and fuel yourself. Chase your dreams and take care of your baby. Leave these mother fuckers right in the damn dust if you have to. Do you understand me?"

"Yes ma'am." I said as I wiped the tears from my face and blew my nose. It was almost as if I wore that burden like a t-shirt. I took on the role of taking care of my siblings before I was old enough to know what it was so it was second nature to me but now that I had Harlym, I was more cautious about what I involved myself in with others. I stood up as Porsha walked towards me. I had to prepare myself for whatever with this bitch. We have had our share of rumbles. Caught off guard, she hugged me.

"I ain't know you felt like we have burdened you. I'll do my part to lighten the load." Porsha said as she kissed my cheek. "On the real though. You do too much crying to be a thug. The shit is ridiculous." We all laughed as my phone binged. It was a message from Mr. Handsome.

Him: thank u 4 earlier beautiful. u single?

Me: Yes. Are you single?

Him: yea. I wanna see you.

Me: When?

Him: wenever u free

Me: Meet me at Mo's on President Street at 7:00pm tomorrow night; your treat. Be safe out. Goodnight.

Him: U got dat.

"Who got you smiling like that? Pete?" Aunt Babs asked.

"She got a new boo Auntie." Porsha teased.

"How you know who it is?" I asked appalled.

"Bitch, I know you! We're damn near twins hoe!"

"Yup, it's him and his name is Dollar Bill."

"As long as he got some dollar bills." Aunt Babs said.

"We'll see. But I gotta go folks. I gotta go home and shower so I can grab a coffee and get on the road at 6am."

"I'm not going to tell you what to do but please be careful on that highway. I want you to go back and finish your degree and start chasing your dreams." Aunt Babs.

"Already registered. I'm going back in Spring Semester. I'm almost done with this." I responded and gave them some love before I left. Apart of that was true. I did register for school and I was going back to finish. I just did not know when I was going to stop these runs. Maybe, Dollar Bill will slow me down. I smiled at the thought.

Chapter Twelve

Checking my watch, I noticed it was 7:15pm. I had already shown up at 6:45pm just not to be late. So, after 30 minutes waiting and 3 glasses of water, I was ready to go. I pulled a twenty out of my purse for the waiter and gathered my belongings. On my way out the door, Mr. Handsome was coming in the door.

"You're late." I snapped.

"I know Babe. Work was crazy." He said with a straight face. "Can you give me a chance to make it up to you?"

"How?" I said rolling my eyes.

"Come on." He said and begin walking out the door. I followed him closely. "Where'd you park?" He asked.

"Why? Why can't we take your car? I don't feel like driving."

"My car is dirty from work. I can just drive your car." He negotiated.

"Cool. Come on. I'm in the parking lot."

"Why the fuck are you parking in the parking lot? This shit high. Probably like $50 an hour."

"It's only $40 for 3 hours."

"Only?"

"For the safety of my car? Yes, that's a small price to pay."

"Already." He shook his head like he was pondering something. I was lost in my own thoughts too tho. Yeah, nigga. I ain't no cheap bitch who impressed by your cash because I got my own ends so you gotta take care of me different. I smiled and he just glanced at me. I unlocked my car and popped the trunk to put my purse in. He got in the driver's side and it made me frown. Once I got in, I realized that the car hadn't been started.

"What's the problem?"

"You didn't give me the key."

"There isn't a key. It's push start."

"Oh shit. I'm geeking." He giggled.

"It's cool. Next time, open my door though before you get in. It's common courtesy and gentleman like."

"My bad. I was cold. But you got that." He responded and instantly, I frowned upon the thought of having to teach him how to treat me. I reclined my seat a bit and turned my seat warmer on. Soon, I had dozed. After not getting any sleep, then driving to Philly and back, I was due for some rest. I felt a tap on my thigh and when I opened my eyes, we were parked by the water in Fells Point. I grabbed my phone and immediately texted Porsha and Lilly.

Me: Dollar Bill. Fells Point. Near Pavillion. My Car.

Porsha: Bet

Lilly: Be Careful. Love you.

Me: Love you more!

I put my phone down and turned my body around so that I was sitting facing him.

"Sooo...What's up?" I asked as he rolled up.

"You tell me."

"Well first thing first. It's no smoking in my car period and as strong as that weed is, I need you never roll it in my car again. My daughter isn't exposed to those types of scents." I said annoyed. I was ready for this date to be over with. It wasn't really my style.

"You are right. My bad. I should have asked you." He said before pausing. "Let's go to the casino."

"Okay. Cool." I said as I sat the seat up and sat forward. I picked up my phone and texted my sisters as I drove.

Me: Not feeling the nigga but headed downtown to the casino.

Porsha: Bitch, act like you do because you need some dick. Some new dick because Pete ain't giving you none of that dick soooooo yeah Bitch!

Lilly: Call it a night if you ain't feeling him. Trust your vibe. Let me know if you need me to come and meet you.

Me: I'm going to go so I can see how much money the nigga working with.

Porsha: My Bitch!

Lilly: Be careful please.

Me: Bet. Love yall.

"I think that's smart that you have someone that you text to let know that you're okay." He said and I tensed up assuming he'd been reading my messages. I was over the entire night at this point. I wasn't sure if he could tell or not, but I really didn't care at this point. I realized then why I hated dating.

"You were reading my messages?" I asked irritated.

"Naw. I just notice that every time we move or stop, you start texting and then put you phone up. I think that's smart. Every woman should move that way. It's too much going on with women getting snatched and shit not to let someone know you're okay."

"Thank you but no one is snatching my fat ass."

"Shiddd. It's niggas out here that love big girls. Then, you sexy as shit. You are definitely snatchable." He responded. "Don't call yourself fat again. That sounds like some low self-esteem shit. You carry yourself well. You're fly as shit. Your attitude a little funky, but that's something you can work on. Plus, I like a little spice. I'd say you're perfect just the way you are."

"Awww. Why aren't you sweet? I didn't know you had it in you. But I don't have esteem issues. I just state facts." I lied. I knew I dressed nice and kept myself pampered well, but I hated everything about my weight gain. In fact, I hadn't felt beautiful about it since my pregnancy, and that was because of Pete.

"Facts? Hmm. I see it different." He responded as we pulled into the parking lot of the casino.

"Interesting. I have to change into my sneakers first."

"That's cool. I can stand outside and smoke while you do that. But let me open your door before you start geeking."

"That is not geeking. That is making it a requirement to be treated as a woman. Nothing less."

"I respect that." He said as he opened my door. I made sure to put a little switch in my walk as I made my way to my trunk. I popped the trunk and took my bank card and license out of my purse and tucked it in my bra. I switched out of my heels into my 990s and they complemented my outfit well.

"Okay, I see you trying to be like me."

"Yeah right. These are old. Yours are fresh. You're definitely trying to be like me. That's cool though."

"Shiddd. They look fresh to me." He said smirking while checking me out. "Where is your purse?"

"Where is my purse?" I asked with a puzzled look on my face.

"Yeah, I don't want to go in there and blow all of my money." He said as he started pulled out stacks of money in rubber bands. If my eye could have illuminated, they definitely would have.

"Oh okay." I opened the trunk again and reached in for my fanny pack. "Here you go." I turned around to give him the fanny pack and he kissed me. Dead smack on the lips. I was caught by surprise, but his lips were so soft. I kissed him back and when I stepped back to catch a breath, I realized that he smelled so good. My hormones began to jump rapidly. "Ummm...What was that?"

"A kiss woman. Now come on." He smacked my ass. I blushed as I licked my lips and followed him into the casino. Once we passed the entrance and got casino cards, it was a wrap. I had the most fun I had in my life on a date. Usually when I came to the casino, it was with my sisters or other family members. We would also lose a lot of money. It would be all in fun though so we wouldn't care. That was not the case tonight though. After we got our cards, Dollar Bill reached in his pocket and pulled out two stacks of money. He handed me one and he kept the other for himself. We started at the slot machines. At the first set of machines, I slid in 3 twenties and won $180. Mr. Handsome on the other hand was not having the best luck I'd saw him lose at least $200. I suggested another slot where he was a little more successful. Again, I made almost five times what I bet.

"I ain't got no luck on these slots. Let us go play the tables."

"I've never played the tables but I'm down." I said excitedly. I didn't count the money he'd given me, but I was already richer than when he handed it to me, so I was having a great time. His company was fun as well.

Before we went to the counted his money. He was down to $600. I counted my money as well and was surprised that I had $1650. I handed him $525.

"What's that for?" He asked.

"Five hundred twenty-five dollars."

"I know what it is for. Why you give it to me?"

"For you to play the tables. You made sure I had money when I came in and you are down on your playing money so it's only right that I return your gesture. Now we have the same amount of playing money." I said.

"I like your style." He said as he nodded his head and looked at me as if he was deep in thought.

"Right." I said cutting the romantics. "Let's go play the tables playboy." Table after table, he played but he loved that blackjack table. I played some but I watched him mostly because he was like a natural at it. He turned that $1125 into $4500 within hours. It was now 3am and though I had a run to make at 10am, I wasn't ready for the night to end. After I literally had to pull him away from the table, we sat and order pizza. He ordered some Remy 1738 but I had water.

"You don't drink." He asked.

"Nope."

"And you don't smoke?"

"Nope."

"Do you do any other recreational drugs?"

"Nope."

"Damn!' He smiled. Like nostalgia, it seemed as if I had seen his smile before. "So, I got a saint."

"You know every saint was once a sinner, right?"

"If you say so. Where are you from because where I am from, girls – excuse me – women as yourself are far and few. Makes me happy I met you."

"They aren't as scarce as you think. There are plenty of diamonds. You gotta remember that diamonds are quality. So, even when they are not shining, their worth does not decrease. Rhinestones – the ones guys chase – are shiny most times but ain't worth shit."

"And you're smart. Yeah, I got the full package."

"Oh, that's what YOU got?"

"I mean unless someone else got you, but I could have sworn you told me that you were single."

"I am very single but the only person that *has me* is my daughter."

"I hear that. I don't have a problem earning my spot." He smiled again. That smile did something to me. "Can I have a kiss?"

"Why?" I asked as I was caught off guard.

"Because your lips are as soft as they look, and I want to kiss them. Last time, I stole a kiss and I don't know if you liked that very much."

"Honestly, I'm not a kisser. But yes, you can kiss me."

"Meet me halfway." He said looking me directly in the eye and I can't lie; it made me nervous a little. We both leaned in across the table and kissed for what seemed like forever. Or at least that is how my back felt. I enjoyed the kiss, but I was happy to sit down. I made a mental note to start taking my ass to the gym and eating healthier. "I like you." He smiled.

"I'm enjoying this date too, but I have to work in a few hours so we gotta wrap this up."

"Let me hit the bathroom and then we can dip. I'll pay for the food when I get back."

"Cool." I smiled as he walked off. I pulled out my phone for the first time of the night. I had 3 missed calls and 7 texts. I looked and saw that the calls and texts were from Porsha and Lilly worried about if I was okay. I had one text from Pete ten minutes prior.

Pete: Hey D. Are you up? I just need to talk.

Me: Is something wrong with Harlym? Is it important? I am on a date but I can step off and call you.

Pete: Naw. She is sleeping. Everything is good. Enjoy yourself. Hit me when you get in so I can know you are okay.

Me: Will do.

I looked up and noticed Mr. Handsome walking back to the table. The waiter brought us the bill which was $45.50. He left a fifty-dollar bill on the table as we prepared to leave, and I think my blood pressure went up. I reached in my bra, where I had kept my money and dropped another fifty on the table.

"What was that for?" he asked.

"Always tip twenty percent or better." I responded. "Do that cheap shit when you are alone."

"I covered the bill. How is that being cheap?"

"Nothing. Don't worry about it. I handled it."

"Naw. Don't do that." He grabbed my arm gently and pulled me towards him as we walked. He put his arm around my shoulders. "Explain it to me. I thought leaving the change was the tip."

"Imagine being on your feet waiting tables all day. You have to serve an average of 3 tables an hour for eight hours. Walking back and forth and standing on your feet consistently. Doesn't matter how many tables, your pay is still four dollars an hour. Making your base pay for the day $32. Would you be happy with that?"

"Why they only getting $4? Ain't it labor laws or some shit they can sue them for? Like I'm not understanding?"

"Waitresses and Waiters are paid like two to four dollars an hour because in their profession, their tips are how they make their money. So, imagine you not being tipped all day or being tipped poorly; especially when you are providing great customer service. Used and abused; that's how they feel."

"I don't get it. I will let you handle that part moving forward. I ain't know it was a rule to tipping."

"It is but who said there was going to be another date?"

"There is definitely going to be a second date." He said after he opened my car door. Meaning even if I had to teach him a thing or two, it's cool because he catches on fast and he was teachable. I appreciated that.

"I hear you. Wake me up when we get to your car. I am tired and I gotta travel all the way home."

"What area do you live in?" He asked and I thought about telling him the truth, but I decided against it.

"Columbia."

"Oh, damn. We could grab a room or something until the morning then we could part ways. I'm not ready for this night to be over."

"I'm cool with that." I blurted out before even really giving the suggestion any thought. "What about your car? I don't want you to get towed."

"Naw, my car is good. I'm going to text my son to go get it."

"You have a son old enough to drive?"

"He just a youngin I call my son for real. He good people though."

"Oh Okay. Cool. What hotel?"

"My spot up on Pulaski. . ."

"Excuse me? I'm not staying in a single mother fucking place on no mother fucking Pulaski. We can go right in Fells Point to the hotel. It's only $150 a night."

"Well if you knew where you wanted to go, why did you ask me?"

"I wanted to see what your taste was like. You failed miserably." We both giggled.

"Well, I don't usually like to go to hotels unless I'm alone just on some chill shit and the ones on Pulaski let me smoke my weed in peace so yeah."

"Understood. I'm going to teach you how to smoke when you are at a nice hotel."

"How would you know?"

"You are not the first smoker I've dealt with. Me and him were together well over 10 years so you better believe I know all the tricks to the trade."

"Your daughter's father?"

"Nope. He's a saint for real in that aspect." I giggled and wondered what Pete wanted to talk about. He pulled into the Royal Farms parking lot.

"Do you want anything?" He asked.

"Yes, some ice and a Pepsi."

"That's it?"

"Yup." I answered as he hopped out the car to go inside. I called Pete while he was inside, but I got no answer, so I decided to text him.

Me: I tried to call you but got no answer. Please call when you wake up.

I put my phone down as Mr. Handsome made his way back to the car. We made our way to the hotel. After a long day, I hopped in the shower to wash the stress and fun of the day off of me. I stepped out of the shower and was startled that Mr. Handsome was sitting on top of the toilet seat smoking a blunt.

"You could have done that in the room."

"I ain't want the people to get to tripping and try to put us out or some shit because they smell it."

"That's why I brought the spray in here and put the wet towel to the door. Hand me my towel please." I said.

"Do you feel like I invaded your space?"

"Yes. I really do."

"That wasn't what I meant to do. Should I just get my own room?"

"No, just announce you're there or something."

"You got that." He responded with a nod of his head as I sashayed to the bed. He was definitely going to fall in love with all of this woman. I dried myself off and laid a fresh towel on the bed so I could lotion myself down. "Can I help you?" He asked.

"Sure. Wash your hands first." I said and he paused.

"You are really a trip. Do you know that?"

"I've been told that a lot throughout my life."

"It's cool though. I like it." He said as he began massaging lotion into my thighs. What started off as a nice gesture, turned into a night of passionate love making. So much love making that I fell asleep. When I awoke, Mr. Handsome was not beside me. It was also 10:30am. I was running late. I was always on time. I prided myself on that. Frustrated, I scanned the room for all of my belongings. Everything seemed in place. Mr. Handsome and his belongings were gone. I did not have time to think about where he went. I had to get going. I hopped in the shower and washed away my sins from the morning thoroughly, but I reminisced on how amazing the sex was. Up until now, Pete was the only person who made me feel catered to during sex. Mr. Handsome was definitely one for the books. Reality slapped me. *Damn! I just fucked this man and do not even know his real name!* I got dressed and grabbed my belongings. I noticed that he left two stacks under my keys. Oh, great. Now, I am a damn prostitute.

Chapter Thirteen

It had been almost six months since that date with Mr. Handsome. In that time, one of Pete's drivers were murdered so he was driving more until he could find a new driver. Nita, Sharif's mother, was a completely different story. She thought that she was going to live this luxurious lifestyle and not work for a dime of it. Their marriage was falling to pieces. I am not going to say I was happy about it, but I'd be lying if I told you that I was sad. However, because I believed that children never had anything to do with what happens between their parents, I never stopped being there for Reef. In fact, lately, he had been staying with me. Nita would request to get him for a day or two here and there but at this point it had become far and few. Tyrik, her and Pete's oldest son, was a momma's boy and refused to leave Nita's side. Which was cool with me because I wasn't close to Tyrik like I was to Reef.

I hadn't completely stopped doing runs, but I had slowed down drastically. Now, I only did a job every other Saturday. It was enough for me to pay my bills, put a little money in my savings, take care of Harlym & Reef on my end so that the burden was less on Pete. I even paid my tithes every Sunday. I figured GOD had been really watching over me and looking out for me something serious. The least I could do was catch a sermon via YouTube and pay my tithes to that one church that made me feel at home. I had even started building on my estate for Harlym if I lost my life for any reason. Financially, I was the most responsible I'd ever been. I was genuinely in a place where my life wasn't perfect, but I was proud of myself and where I am. Pete and I had a much better relationship now and an authentic friendship that I valued greatly. I began taking heed to the lessons he taught me. The main one was not looking like more money than I had. First thing I did was sell my Cadillac and bought myself a Chevrolet Cruze. It was much more cost efficient for gas and maintenance. I absolutely loved it.

Another thing that had changed was that I had not heard from Mr. Handsome. He did not reach out and neither did I. It was a night of fun, but I did not see that we could become more than that.

That was until that one Thursday. I made my way to pick Sharif up from his after-school program where he went after his head start class. As I drove to the school, I noticed Mr. Handsome standing in front of a store close to where I had met him. I had 30 mins to go before Sharif was due to be picked up from after school program, so I decided to spin the block. I looked back at Harlym who was completely knocked out and figured it was perfect timing to do a little pop up. As I pulled up on him, I honked my horn and we locked eyes. I pulled over to the corner and waited for him to come to the car. I looked in my rearview mirror to see what was taking him so long and noticed that he was in a heated exchange with a female. She appeared attractive under the damage that obvious alcoholism had done to her. He made his way down the street and she watched him with sadness in her eyes. Immediately, I felt sad for her. I knew that feeling her eyes spoke too well.

"Hello beautiful!" He said as he adjusted the seat breaking my stare at his friend. Suddenly, I was no longer happy to see him.

"Hey." I responded flatly.

"What's wrong?"

"Who was that girl?"

"My god sister. She mad because I am not giving her a couple dollars. I just gave her twenty dollars this morning. I am not a bank machine. All she gonna do is cop percs with it anyway. I'm not contributing to her habit." I listened and even though it did not sit right with my gut, I went with it. I mean, he did not owe me any lies, right? We would see.

"Oh wow. I kinda know what that feels like." I looked up in the mirror and the girl was now sitting on the step of the store talking to another young man crying.

I knew how it felt to struggle with addiction. I had finally surrendered myself to GOD's will, gotten a sponsor, and was working the necessary steps of my recovery.

"Fuck her and that dumb shit. How have you been? Where have you been? What was wack? My dick or the head?" He asked and I slapped his arm.

"My daughter is back there. Watch your mouth!"

"Awww man. I apologize. I wouldn't be talking like that around your kid. I really apologize."

"It's cool. You ain't know. Anyway, I enjoyed myself the entire night. When you did not hit me, I assumed you were no longer interested so I just went on about my business."

"Naw, I lost my phone that morning for real so when I got a new one, I made a whole new Facebook page and couldn't find you."

"Well, I don't know why because my name on there is my real name. Unlike you, whose real name I do not even know. That was another thing. I ain't want you to think that was my style for real. Like I was a jump off or some shit."

"Mannnn, are you serious? I ain't look at you like that at all. My real name is William Jeffries though."

"You're lying."

"I'm dead ass serious. That's my name." He pulled his wallet out of his pocket and opened it to his identification card, and I read his name *William Ronreco Jeffries* in my mind. I made a mental note of his address too. "This old but I can't find my license, so I just carry this. Always gotta have ID on me."

"Okay. Cool. Well, I gotta run. I'll catch up with you when I can."

"What? We not gonna exchange numbers or nothing? You cold."

"You didn't ask. I didn't know. I really gotta go though. I have to pick my nephew up from after school program." Before I could think, the lie rolled right off my tongue, but it helped that Sharif called me Aunt Diamond.

"What school?"

"Elementary school on Lakewood. Two blocks from here."

"Can I ride with you?"

"I don't think that's a good idea."

"Why not? He gotta meet auntie's boyfriend one day."

"Boyfriend?"

"Yes, boyfriend. And I'm jealous so I don't want you around no niggas."

"Oh, that's a tuff titty because outside of my roommate and my two sisters, everyone close to me are males. My best friend is even a male." That was not all the way a lie. Pete was like my best friend and outside of Lilly & Porsha, Rell & Lee were my only friends.

"As long as they know their place."

"I hear you. Are you sure you want to ride?" I asked. In reality, I didn't know if I was asking him or myself because I knew Sharif would tell Pete that a guy was in the car.

"Yeah. Come on." He said. Instantly, a cold shiver went through my body and I looked around as I felt eyes on me. I had gotten used to that happening to me lately, so I just blamed it on paranoia. I pulled the car.

"Cool." I pulled off but not before checking my rearview mirror. The girl must had left in the middle of midst of us conversing. "Your girlfriend dipped."

"Naw. Sadly, she ain't going anywhere until she gets some money out of me. She probably in the bar getting a drink. That ain't my girl though. I just look out for her because she's like family and my mother asked to make sure she's okay. You can go ask her. She'll still be right there."

"I believe you." I said as I pulled up to the school. I turned off the car and prepared to wake Harlym up. *Damn!* I thought. I had not thought about the fact that I didn't even know this man for real and I was about to leave him in my car unattended. I decided to text one of my homegirls instead hoping and praying that she had allowed her daughter to attend after school program today.

> *Me: Hey Renae. Are you at the school?*
>
> *Renae: Yeah. Wassup?*
>
> *Me: Can you bring Sharif out with you? I am in the car but Harlym sleep and I really don't want to wake her?*
>
> *Renae: Cool.*

I breathed a sigh of relief. I was slipping for real. I looked over at Dollar, as that's what I decided that I was going to call him, and he looked as if he was pondering over a text.

"What's wrong?" I asked.

"Nothing." He responded flatly.

"Auntieeeee!" Sharif said as he opened the car door.

"Hey Baby!" I responded before looking for Renae. I rolled my window down. "Thanks, Renae!"

"No problem Boo!" She responded.

"How was school?" I asked Sharif.

"It was cool. I have a girlfriend."

"Boy you are in head start. You don't know anything about a girlfriend." I responded.

"Shiddddd. Do Your thing lor man." Dollar interrupted.

"Ayyyeee. No & no!" I said loudly.

"What?" He looked surprised.

"What? For one, do not cuss around my kids. Ever. They are not exposed to that kind of language. For two, he does not have a girlfriend. All he has is his schoolbooks."

"You right. My bad." He said. I introduced him as my friend to Sharif and they shook hands. Then, we talked a little as I dropped him back off. "When am I going to see you again?" He asked.

"The next time you take me on a date."

"Okay, okay. We gotta go eat and chop it up. What are you doing this weekend?"

"Going to Philly."

"Damn. No invite?"

"You can come." I responded before thinking.

"Cool. One day or a couple days?"

"Friday to Sunday."

"Rd. Bet. I'm serious."

"Me too."

"Okay. Gotta hit the mall and get right."

"Grab me something."

"You got that." He said and reached over to give me a kiss. I slid my cheek to him. "Okay, Okay. Let me get out here and get to it because I'm going to need a couple bags fucking – I mean messing with you."

"As long as you know." I said and giggled as he kissed my cheek. He hopped out the car and patted the hood. I drove off and made my way home thinking about him. His vibe was weird, but we connected. Or Maybe I just wanted to not be alone. Whatever it was, I was going to enjoy it. Pete's phone call broke me from my thoughts. I rolled my eyes up in my head and answered the car phone.

"Yes sir. How can I help you?"

"Hey Beautiful. How'd Sharif do in school today?"

"I'm not sure how he behaved. I did not go in and get him. Renae brought him out for me because Harlym was sleep and I didn't want to wake her. However, he says his has a girlllfriendddd." I laughed as I drug the word out girlfriend.

"Aww man! I thought we'd at least make it to second grade."

"I know right. Your baby is growing up."

"Our baby is growing up."

"You and Nita's baby is growing up." I snapped and instantly regretted saying it. I checked the mirror and thanked GOD that Sharif had fallen asleep. Pete was silent. "Have you talked to Nita lately?" I asked.

"Naw. I talked to her mother. She wanted to get Sharif, but I told her that I'd get back to her. I wanted to run it pass you first so I can see what you thought."

"I don't think that my opinion should matter. However, since I know you will insist, I believe that her parents shouldn't suffer for her lack of parenting. Sharif deserves to know his family like he knows my family."

"You're right. See, I felt I'd be protecting him from all that foolishness by just keeping him around good energy where he feels safe."

"Naww. Give them a chance."

"Thanks, beautiful."

"No problem. Drive safe." We hung up the phone and I carried on with my day as normal; homework, dinner, baths, and a movie. It was our routine. However usually after the kids fall asleep so do I. Not tonight. I made it my business to find my clothing for this weekend and have my bag packed. I never packed a bag because I usually came back the same day I went up. This weekend would be a bit different and I was looking forward to it. I hadn't been out of town with a man since Pete and that was before Harlym was born.

The rest of the weekdays went pass fast and it was finally Friday. Pete was picking the kids up from daycare and school, so I had free time to get pampered and catch up with my sisters. I sat in Shannon's chair as she slayed my hair and caught up with my sisters.

"Bitchhhhh, it's really been forever. You and Pete done went back to being a family and shit." Porsha said as she rolled her eyes.

"Bitch please. We are not playing house or anything. We co-parent. That's all."

"Yeah, and fuck from time to time."

"Actually. The last person and next person I'm going to fuck is Dollar."

"What Dollar bitch? Dollar Bill?" Porsha sat forward in her chair.

"Yes, bitch. Dollar Bill."

"Dollar Bill from Monument Street?" Shannon asked.

"Yes ma'am. Why? Spill the tea Bitch." I said.

"Well bitch I know he was fucking with the bitch Pearl from Port Street, but he literally uses her ass as a damn punching bag. Now I don't know if he still fucks with her, but he was recently. The bitch drink 40s like a nigga and pop more percs than a little bit but in a sick, twisted way, he really loves her." Shannon said shaking her head.

"Wayment. So, you think he still fucking this bitch?" I asked as my mind thought back to the girl with the sad eyes. I instantly shook the thought away and refocused on the conversation.

"And if you don't know, who the fuck you gotta call to find out?" Porsha asked before Shannon could even answer my question.

"To my knowledge, yes, he's not only still fucking with her but still fucking with her too." Shannon answered.

"Fucking clown. That's cool. He wants to play. I can play better."

"And bitch you better cash the fuck out too." Porsha said sternly.

"Call me what you want but I think you should just leave him alone baby sis." Lilly said softly.

"You right. I probably should." I put my head down. I can't lie, I was a little disappointed.

"Bitch, get your coins, then bow out gracefully." I pondered how it could go either way. He wasn't my man and I wasn't his woman so what was the problem being friends? My phone rang startling me.

"Yes sir?" I asked sarcastically as I answered the phone.

"I have a question and do not lie to me." Pete responded.

"Pete, who the fuck are you to lie to?" I asked annoyed.

"Who the fuck is this clown you had in the car with my kids?" He yelled. Damn! Sharif's little snitching ass told on me. Pete was mad and I loved every single minute of it. I thought long and hard about my answer.

"My man." I responded maliciously.

"Your man? Oh, yeah? I wish you the best and you can do you. However, keep that nigga away from my fucking kids."

"First and foremost, nigga, I don't need your fucking permission. I know I can do me. I can respect your wishes with Sharif because that's not my child but you're not going to tell me what to do with my fucking daughter."

"You got me fucked up. I will take my fucking daughter if you think that you're ever going to put her in any unsafe or unsure setting or situation." He said and I knew he was mad because he never cursed regularly, let alone repeatedly.

"So, by unsafe you mean around another man other than her parent? Someone's jealous."

"By unsafe, I mean around a fucking drug dealer and killer. Stop fucking playing with me Bitch." I was appalled by how much he knew considering he really stays out the way.

"Nigga, you're tripping. Bye Pete!" I hung up. I knew he meant business because he had never talked to me like that before in the entirety of us knowing each other. I understood where he was coming from but why the fuck wouldn't I protect my daughter. I ain't let that damper my mood. Pete would be mad if I moved on with a saint. He is just perfectly fine with me being by myself. Naw, I am done with that. Even if me and Dollar was nothing more than good friends who fuck, I was tired of being alone. No longer was I going to be afraid to live a little; or a lot.

Chapter Fourteen

The time had come to prepare for my run, but I was extremely excited for this trip. I looked forward to relaxing and to spend time with a man. The thought of having sex had me extremely horny, but I'm not going to lie and say I wasn't thinking about Pearl. Did he lie to me or does the streets just not know his business like they claimed to? I began to take roll my bag to the elevator in my building, but I checked my mail on the way out. There was a bunch of junk mail, some things for Trina, and two letters for me. I placed Trina's mail back in the mailbox before opening my own. My first letter was a conditional offer of employment from Johns Hopkins Hospital for a position I had applied for a few months prior. I could've cried tears of joy. Next was a letter from an inmate named Lester Royal. Who the fuck is that? I opened the letter and an instant chill went over my body when I realized the letter was from Devon. How the fuck do you know where I live nigga? I made a mental note to start looking for a new place. I was curious as to what he could possibly want with me.

My Precious Diamond,

I know you are surprised to hear from me. I did not plan on writing you but word on the street is that you haven't had enough of minding my fucking business. Who the fuck told you to find Meka somewhere to stay? I was in the middle of teaching that bitch a lesson and here come your fat ass trying to save the day. She is still going to learn though. I bet you that. Now, so are you. If you want to mind my business, put some money on my accounts. That is the least you can do since you ain't ever did shit but spend my money up. Now you are living large. Riding around in the Cadillac I bought. Moving shit for my plug. I should have been let you get your head knocked off. Naw, I love you too much to do that. You will pay; for interfering in my shit with Meka – MY BABYMOTHER, for not having enough gratitude for all I've done for you to send me a couple dollars, and especially for having another fucking bastard with that bitch ass nigga. What the fuck you thought I wouldn't find out? Bitch I am going to see you. Sooner than you think. Do not think your new little boyfriend can save you either because he can't bitch. I will not let you know when I'm coming but you'll definitely feel it. Have that pussy shaved like I like it because I'm getting some before I send you to your maker.

See You Soon,

Daddy (You Still Call Me That, Okay?) LOL!

My entire mood shifted. Not just because I was scared, but I feared for my daughter's safety. As much as I wanted to be, I was not with her 24 hours a day so I couldn't assure that she'd always be safe. I wanted to put that to the side for now. Devon had at least seven years and as much as he was an asshole, he was not a snitch. I shook my head in an attempt to refocus my energy, but it was hard to. I had to show Pete this letter, but it would have to wait. I mean we still had about six years before we would see his ass. All I kept thinking about is Devon coming after me. I was not scared. I just felt off point. I mean this nigga knew exactly where I lived; down to the apartment number. That frightened me severely. I made my way to pick up Dollar and we got on the road to Philly.

"What are you thinking about?" Dollar asked.

"Nothing important." I lied.

"Are you sure because I'm a good person to talk to?" He insisted

"I'm sure but no, thank you."

We pulled into the turnabout of the hotel in Jersey and I searched for valet so they could park the car. *Never shit where you eat!* I decided not to stay in Philly since I had to attend to my business there. Once we had our bags and were checked in, I went straight to the room and laid down. Before I could say anything, I was sleep. When I awake it felt like it was hours later but when I did awake, Dollar was holding me closely. I snuggled up under him and it felt so good. Just as I was about to doze back off, I felt him stretch and wiggle a little bit.

"How'd you sleep beautiful?"

"I slept well actually. Very comfortably."

"That's what's up." He said as he massaged my nipple from behind. I could feel his hard on pressing against my butt. I got up and hopped in the shower, assuring I'd be nice and fresh. Before I could completely dry myself off, he pushed me back on the bed and started devouring my vagina like he was starving. After giving me multiple orgasms via oral sex, he jumped in the shower himself. My hormones were jumping, and he found out just how much when he returned to the room. We had sex repeatedly and soon I forgot about Devon and the bullshit that came along with him. Afterwards, we just laid there. Pearl came to my mind.

"Who is Pearl?" I asked and let out a long sigh.

"My first love." He began. "We've been off and on since we were kids. I will probably love her forever, but she got some demons that she has to deal with. We have no communication at all currently. In fact, because of you. Someone told her that they have been seeing me with you. We got into it and got physical. I do not want to deal with that. That is not the man I am. I was raised right by my mother and I do not want to be anything less than what she raised me to be for real. I want something peaceful, no stress. Like, look at how we are chilling. I love this. I have never been outside of Baltimore unless I was going to a jail in another city of Maryland. This means a lot to me. There is a lot that I haven't experienced but I'm down for creating more memories with you." When he finished, I was like 'Pearl, who?'

"That's good to know." I said playing it cool. I liked him a lot already. "Let's go make some memories then. Just like that, we had a ball all weekend. We went to different restaurants, local stores, entertainment spots, and even a nice lounge. We really enjoyed ourselves. He wasn't a morning person, so I had arranged the perfect times to do my runs. I followed the instructions I'd received from Charisma's men precisely and all went well. We had a ball and I handled business. It was time to head home.

"Did you enjoy yourself?" He asked as we pulled off.

"I did." I said as I beamed.

"That's what's up. Look, I was serious about being your man. You give me a different vibe that I have never felt before. I don't want to let that go and I'm willing to do whatever I have to in order to make you happy and keep you happy. You'll be provided for and protected. Both you and your daughter. You can bet that. I have four kids of my own and I take good care of mine. We can get them all together and hit the beach or something."

"That would be nice." I agreed.

"Yeah, let us set up that up. How much are your bills monthly?"

"What bills?"

"All of your bills. What's the total of your monthly bills?"

"Ummm..." I calculated my bill in my head. "A little over $2000 a month." At the next red light, he went in his pocket and counted out some bills off his stack.

"This is $2500. Moving forward, I pay your bills. You use your money for whatever you desire."

"As good as that sounds, I can't accept this."

"What you not used to being taken care of?" He asked confused.

"Actually, that's all I'm used to. However, I can't take you up on your offer of being your woman because my past is still haunting me right now. I wouldn't put you in the middle of that."

"What you still fucking with your baby father?"

"Absolutely not. My ex is locked up right now but he's sending death threats to me and my daughter."

"What your baby father doing about it?"

"He doesn't know. I'm going to talk to him about it but he's doing so well with his life. I don't want to uproot it with my shit. I just wish my ex would go away. I'm just trying to live and be happy." I put my head down.

"What's his name?" "Devon Miller. Everyone calls him Dev."

"Devon Miller from Milton Ave?"

"Yes!"

"I'll handle him. You just handle the bills with that money I gave you. We in this together and I got you." He said and I felt relieved.

"Okay." I responded before I got comfortable in my seat and fell asleep as he drove.

Chapter Fifteen

Darling, I was in Heaven. Dollar and I went on dates every few days. He bought me flowers often. I had to tell him repeatedly what my favorites were, but it was the thought that counted. He kept his word on paying my bills. I was thriving in my new position at the hospital. I got some much-needed quality time with Harlym. Everything was finally in place and I was completely at peace. I enjoyed it because I knew it was not long before something would throw me a curveball. I was right too. One night we went to dinner at Mo's Seafood. I knew whatever he needed to discuss was urgent. I just did not know what. My father used to say, *if it cannot be discussed on the phone, that means someone is gone or must go.* I hoped he was coming to tell me that Devon was dead. I did not get my hopes up for that because the streets would have been buzzing by now and Porsha would have been on my line. I looked up and saw Dollar coming towards me.

"Hey baby." He said as he sat down.

"Hey lover."

"How are you feeling?"

"Anxious! What's going on?"

"Let's order some food first."

"I already ordered our food."

"What did you get me?"

"Oyster Rockefeller, catfish nuggets, & a crab cake with a lemonade."

"Okay, okay. You think you know me."

"I do." I said and smiled. "It's a habit of mine to learn the people close to me."

"Well, let's get down to business beautiful."

"I'm listening." I said and I was completely tuned in and paying attention.

"We're close to getting your boy. He's smarter than I thought so he maneuvered our traps so far."

"Kinda figured." I said sadly.

"Don't look down. I got you Bae. That nigga will not lay a finger on you or Harlym. I promise you that."

"Okay." I said sounding as defeated as I felt.

"It's okay Babe. Something more important is pressing though. Take this money and move."

"Move?" I asked confused.

"Move, where?"

"I don't know Dia. But you gotta do it ASAP. Remember you said the black car followed you home and kept popping up different places? All that's connected to nigga that's trying to kill me." He said and I thought back to when I told him those incidents.

"What?" I asked angrily.

"D, you knew exactly who I was and what I did for a living when you met me. This is a part of the game Baby. Just lay low for a few weeks; work and home and everything is going to go back to normal."

"Who's the nigga?"

"I don't even know the niggas names, but I know them when I see them, and I will see them. I refuse to have you and baby girl being in the middle of this shit." Dollar explained.

"So, how does that effect our relationship."

"We have to chill on the dates or being out too much. We have to take down our pictures from social media. And I already told you that you have to move."

"Take our pictures down?"

"Yes, it needs to appear that we've broken up or something, so they won't be focused on you. Don't you know niggas kill the closest thing to a nigga to make him feel it? I couldn't live with myself if anything happened to you or Harlym." He said sounding sincere. *You wouldn't live period. Trust me.* I thought but I just sat there, not saying anything for a minute.

"Don't put handling Devon on the back burner."

"Absolutely not. I got niggas sitting over the jail on him now. Oh, his time is winding down baby girl."

"Cool." I said as I got up to leave.

"Where you going?" He called out to me.

"To move." I yelled back without turning around. What he said made sense but something inside of me would not allow me to believe it. I do not know if it was my trust issues or because the shit was bullshit. Either way, I had to make sure I protected my daughter, so it was time to move. I rode I silence until I pulled in front of my apartment building. I closed my eyes and sat my head back. When I opened my eyes, that same black car with dark tints was parked at the top corner of my block. I pulled my phone out and called Pete. He did not answer but he texted.

Pete: Wassup?

Me: Red Ribbons. White Skies.

Pete: McDonalds on Franklin. 15 Mins Out.

I started my car and made my way to McDonalds. Pete and I had created that code when we were younger. It was strictly for emergencies. I'd only used it once when my father came in the house drunk and ended up beating up on me. Pete came and calmed the situation; including slapping my father up a few times. I was happy he remembered. The meeting location was not that far from me, so I made it there in seven minutes. I circled the lot twice before parking. Pete did the same when he arrived and backed in next to me. I got out and got into his car. I sat there in silence for a minute. I did not know where to start. The tears started to fall uncontrollably.

"What's going on D?" Pete asked concerned.

"I don't even know where to start." I cried

"The beginning and don't skip shit." I did not respond. I went in my purse and gave him the letter from Dev. He read the letter and then looked at the envelope with my address.

"FUCK, D! This is exactly why you should've let me kill him when I had the chance to." I continued to cry silently.

"That's not it." I admitted.

"What else?"

"Dollar is beefing with some niggas and I'm quite sure they know where I live, where I hang, and how my car looks."

"Damn Diamond!" He yelled as he hit the steering wheel. "Do you see the fucking pattern in your choices? You are a mother now D. You're a mother first D. You are a mother first D. You are a fucking mother first."

"I know Peter! Do you know how hard this was for me to come to you?"

"No. Do you know how it feels to want to protect you from them mother fuckers from the jump, but you never listen to me? Do you know how hard it is for you to just show genuine interest in someone that is not like your sorry ass father? I went through all that shit to rid your life of him only for you to date mother fuckers who are EXACTLY like him."

"I'm sorry Pete." I said and put my head down.

"Yes, the fuck you are. Give me your keys." I handed him my car keys. "Your house keys, too." I obliged.

"Take my car and go to Aunt Babs house with the kids. I'll call you with instructions later. Do not talk to anybody about anything. Keep talking to your boyfriend as normal but stray away from any crazy conversations."

"Okay." I did as I was told and went straight to Aunt Babs house. When I had gotten there, the kids were sleep so I crawled unto the air bed with them and dozed off. I woke to my phone ringing, it was Dollar.

"Hello." I answered sounding sleepy.

"Hey. Are you okay?" He asked.

"Yeah. Just have a headache." I responded.

"I need to use your car Bae."

"I don't have my car." I replied flatly.

"Who has your car?"

"What? Why does it matter who has my car?"

"What the fuck you mean? You're my bitch and I just told you what's been going on, so it does matter."

"I'm not your bitch. I'm nobody's bitch. My little brother has my car and I'm sleep so good night." Before he could respond, I hung up and put my phone on Do Not Disturb.

My mind was so busy overthinking that I found it hard to sleep. I tried everything to try to dose off but it just wasn't working. After a few hours, I sat up on the side of the bed and grabbed my phone. The first thing I noticed was that I had 17 missed calls and 5 missed messages; the two most recent calls were from Pete. I called him back.

"Hey. Are y'all sleep?" Pete asked without saying Hello.

"Yes. Do you want us to get up?"

"Naw. I need you to take the kids to your Grandmother and leave your boyfriend your car."

"I haven't even talked to my grandmother in years. Literally, not since the day I was sentenced. I can't just call like I need you, again. It is about niggas, again. I need you to bail me out of trouble, again."

"I talk to your grandmother every single day. She knows you are bringing the kids. She is anxious for her reunion with you. We cannot solve your problems with the kids here. Aunt Babs has the money for you to give to Grandma."

"Okay. We'll leave in the morning."

Chapter Sixteen

I pulled up to my grandmother's front in the van I rented and sat there for a minute before going in. I practiced breathing as I felt I was hyperventilating. Guilt had me choked up like someone was strangling me. I looked in the rear mirror and both Sharif & Harlym were in a deep sleep. I pulled out my phone and called Dollar. Regardless of everything going on, I still liked him a little. Lately things had been rocky because of the situation with the guys he was beefing with but I focused on our good times and there were many of those. He was not all bad and nobody was perfect. I know it was naïve to believe that something could come of us, but I did.

"Heyyyy." He answered.

"Hey baby. I miss you."

"I miss you too. You need the car back?"

"Naw. I'll get it tomorrow. Just calling to check on you."

"I'm good. Where my baby at?"

"Right here sleep. Boutta wake her up so I can take her somewhere where she can enjoy herself."

"Oh Rd. That sounds cool. Call me and let me know if you need me. It's busy out here right now baby."

"Okay. Be careful. I love you."

"I love you more Dia." I hung up.

I hated when he called me Dia. Like who is Dia? I did not have time to focus on that right now. It was time to face the music. I woke my babies up and took them into my grandma's house. She left no room for sadness or guilt to reside. From the minute we stepped foot in her house, it was a celebration. As the evening winded down and it was time for me get back on the road. We had eaten, shopped for the kids, sang, danced, cried, and reminisced. Repeatedly, I apologized but she assured me that all was well between us and that she would do it again if she had to. How could someone who had gone through so much, be so forgiving? She begged to stay one night and get some rest, but I could not. She walked me to the door and handed me a bag that contained of sandwiches, fruit, and waters to travel with. The kids were in bed and it was the perfect time for me to get out of there without them throwing a fit. In my heart, I wanted to stay and just say forget everything that was going on in Baltimore. That is not how I was raised. I always faced my problems head on. Grandma & I hugged for what felt like forever.

"Baby, it's all going to be okay. Do you hear me? I have already prayed about it and I trust GOD to do exactly what he promised. Now, you just keep your head up and do whatever is necessary to protect you and Pete. Do you hear me? I need you to keep him close because something is wrong. I can't quite put my finger on it but he is on edge. I can feel it when he talks to me."

"Yes ma'am. I will. I will not let anything happen to him. I promise. I wish I could stay Grandma. I don't want to go back."

"No! No! No! That is one thing we have never done and will never do. We do not run from our problems. We handle them. Especially the ones we create for ourselves. Do you hear me?"

"Yes ma'am. I love you Grandma." I said as my voice cracked, and the tears began to flow.

"I love you too. Weeping may endure for a night, but joy comes in the morning. Joy is coming baby. Joy is coming. You gotta know you deserve it." She said and dried my eyes.

"I'll see you soon Grandma."

"Indeed, you will." She smiled. "Now, go help your husband."

"Yes ma'am." I giggled. "That's my baby's pretty smile. Kiss Pete's cheek for me."

"I surely will." I made my way back to Baltimore and the long ride alone gave me time to think about everything that was transpiring in my life. Was I really that desperate for love that I had risked my children? Once I reached Downtown, I grabbed a room at the Hyatt. As soon as I went to the room, I laid on the bed and cried. Soon, I was sleep. I was exhausted from driving and life in general. I did not take off my coat or shoes. I must have needed that rest badly because it was the next afternoon when I woke up. Thank GOD I had gotten the room for a few days. I had to pee but of course I grabbed my phone to take in there with me. I had several missed calls from Pete. I called him back immediately.

"Where are you?" He answered the phone. "On Central at the Hyatt. I really needed sleep. I'm sorry." I said apologetically and he breathed a sigh of relief.

"Stay there and do not leave. What's your code?"

"1956" I stated which meant everything was cool and I felt safe.

"Bet. I'm on my way."

"Wait! Pete, what's going on?" I shouted.

"Devon is not in jail. He was released a week ago. The nigga is an informant." My head started spinning. I knew he would come after me. More importantly to me, I wondered why Dollar would lie about having the situation under control after I told him that the nigga threatened my daughter.

"What?"

"You are good for now. He has been staking your house out, so he does not know where you are now which is a good thing. Still must be cautious because he knows your cars; both the Cadillac and the Chevy."

"Yeah. I know. I am going to sleep until you get here. Knock four times."

"Bet." As soon as he hung up, Dollar was calling. Speak of the fucking Devil. I exhaled deeply before answering the phone.

"Hello?"

"Bae, you good?"

"Kind of. Just thinking a lot."

"About what? What's wrong? Talk to me baby."

"About Devon."

"Man, don't let that nigga rent no space in your fucking head. I already told you that I got that shit sewed up. My mans over there just hollered at me earlier and he'll have that wrapped up tonight so you ain't never gotta worry about that nigga again."

"They're in the same jail?"

"Even closer than that. Their cells are right next to each other." He lied with ease.

"Oh Damn. That's what's up. Thanks baby. Where you at? I miss you." My voice weakened as the tears fell.

"Awww Bae. I miss you more. I'm almost done wrapping this beef shit up then everything can go back to normal. Man, I miss the shit out of y'all. Maybe we can take a trip and take the kids somewhere. But you know where I'm at."

"Oh rd. Please be careful out there." I tried my best to sound concerned.

"I will baby. You need anything?"

"Nope. I'm good."

"Cool. Kiss the baby for me."

"Gotchu." I hung up the phone and anger filled my veins.

I picked up my keys and forgot all about laying low. I made my way to Monument street because I had a few things to tell this lying mother fucker. I drove 80mph the entire way there. When I pulled up on him, his eyes got big as if he'd seen a ghost.

"Why the fuck would you lie to me knowing that my daughter was in danger?" I asked as I hopped out the car.

"What the fuck are you even talking about?"

"I'm talking about your lying ass. Your mans on Dev, right?"

"Yeah, I told you that."

"I know you did and you're a mother fucking liar. Devon is home and has been for a week."

"Wait what? How the fuck you know if that's true? You listening to what them dumb ass bitches at the salon be saying. They be loud and wrong as a bitch. Don't know what the fuck they talking about."

"I saw him with my own two eyes nigga." I lied but I know if Pete said it, then it was solid information.

"What? Where?"

"Sitting outside my fucking apartment building last night."

"I told you stop staying there."

"Don't act like you give a fuck because if you did, we would be staying with you; not hopping pillar to post."

"I already told you my situation and that I'm laying low until this shit blow over. I've been staying at my Mother's shit and she ain't going to allow you and Harlym to stay at her house."

"Right and Harlym's mother can't let you hold her car. Give me my keys." At this point, I was just making a scene because I had my spare key in my purse in the car.

"Man go the fuck head. I'm not giving you shit. I asked you earlier if you needed the car when I texted you and you ain't respond so I made plans."

"I don't give a fuck what your plans are. You will not be attending them in my fucking car. Give me my mother fucking keys now. That's the last time I'm asking nicely."

"DDDD!" Someone shouted out and everything moving in slow motion. Turning towards the voice, I glanced at Devon standing across the street with a gun pointed straight at me.

"Get down Dia." He shouted as he bum-rushed me to the ground. His body dropped on top of mine following a hail of bullets. I felt a hot liquid on my stomach and began cussing and fussing in my mind. *I know damn well this mother fucker ain't pissing on me with his scary ass.*

"Im hit baby. Get the gun."

"Huh?" I asked confused as I begin to panic when I saw it was blood and not urine.

"Get the gun off of me." He managed to say. Slowly I rolled his body off me onto the ground. I grabbed his gun, drugs, money and cell phone. I heard sirens approaching so I had to leave. I kissed him quickly and hopped back in the van and drove towards the hotel. As I drove, I took my shirt off that was soaked in blood, wiped as much blood off my breast and stomach as I could, and placed my jacket on and zipped it up. I placed all the bloody stuff in the bag with my leftovers from Grandma's house. I placed his gun, drugs, phone, and money in my purse and snapped it closed. I drove out to a house where my father used to go in Brooklyn Park when he had to get rid of his guns. It had been so long that I was surprised I remembered the way. I knocked on the door. An elderly lady answered the door.

"How can I help you?"

"I'm looking for Ms. Fluff."

"I'm Mrs. Fluff."

"How are you? My name is. . ."

"No need. I know who you are and why you came." She stepped to the side and allowed me to come in pass her. She handed me a sweat suit, a pair of socks, a small bottle of body wash, and a small packet. "Everything else you need is out in the bathroom. Go take a shower. Wet your hair and wash it with this solution in the packet. Use the body wash on your body. It's strong. Make sure your wash your hands and fingernails with it but do not – I repeat DO NOT – get this anywhere near your eyes or inside your vagina or you'll be in a world of trouble. Put everything single thing you touch that isn't nailed down in that metal basket. Once you are finished taking a shower, put the towel, washcloth, toothbrush, toothpaste, and all trash in the metal basket as well."

"Its clothes in the bag with the gun as well."

"I'll handle that. You do what I told you to do." I entered her bathroom and it's as if she expected me. I followed her instructions thoroughly. I scrubbed my body vigorously and dressed in the clothes she gave me once I got out. She even had slippers for me. Do I put my shoes in the basket too?

"Everything in the basket." She yelled from downstairs. What the fuck? I did what I had to do and once I got downstairs, there was Pete sitting there covered in blood completely lost to his own thoughts.

"Baby, what happened?" I said as I went to go towards him, but Mrs. Fluff put her hand up stopping me.

"Baby, he has to clean up then y'all can talk." I stepped back.

"Pete, talk to me please."

"He's gone. Devon. He's gone. I killed him. I had to or he was going to kill you. Which I have no regrets about. However, there is no way I can get away with this. Too many people saw me. There's also a camera right there." He put his head down and I broke down completely.

"I'm so sorry Pete. I'm so sorry." I sobbed but he was unaffected by my cries. Everything he built in his life was ruined because of my bad decisions. There was absolutely nothing I could do to take it back.

"Diamond, I love you more than I've ever loved any other woman in my life outside of my mother. I provided every need you had and catered to your wants even when it was out of my character and went against what I believe in. When you attempted to do it on your own, I always held you down if you fell short. Consistently filling the gap. That shit was never good enough for you. Naw, you have this unhealthy infatuation with following your impulsive decision without considering the consequences. Even if that cost you the things you should value most; self-respect, peace, and principles. I loved you anyway. Praying that one day my love would be enough for you. It never was though. I learned a while ago that it never would be. Devon and your father fucked your head up so bad that it didn't make a difference if I went and shouted, 'I love you' from the rooftops of Paradise, your feelings would be the only thing that matters. If I take care of you, you tolerate me. Well, I have nothing left to give. I have nothing left to give." He got up and left out and I cried profusely. He was right. I was completely selfish and irresponsible in my decision making, ultimately ruining the very man GOD sent to love me. I knew he was going to need his space and I was going to respect that. That was not going to stop me from being there for him. I had no idea how this situation with Devon was going to turn out. Respecting his space, I didn't follow him out to his car. I assumed he forgot something in the car and that is why he left out.

"I'm not one to insert my nose in others business but you need to hold on close to him." Ms. Fluff said breaking me from your thoughts. "I have known him since your father brought him here as a young boy. I have never seen anything other than strength exuding from him. There was a deep sadness and vulnerability in his words and in his eyes today." I listened attentively.

"I got him. How much do we owe you?"

"Pete took care of it already Sweetie. You just go find him and make sure he's okay."

"Find him?" I asked as I realized that about 10 minutes had passed. I got up and looked out the window to see that his car was gone. I went out to the van and noticed a note on the dashboard.

Take care of the kids.

I love you still.

See you in the next life.

Epilogue

I sat down in my seat as the Imam spoke a few words and provided everyone the details of Pete's burial site and repast. So many people filled the Masjid and it had only been two days since his tragic death. I had yet to mourn him because I had to pull this all together so fast to honor his religion. When he left Mrs. Fluff's, that was the last time I saw him alive. A group of kids found him in his car outside of his Mom's old house with a hole in his head and his gun in his hand. Getting an autopsy was against Pete's religion so I accepted that they ruled it a suicide. I did not believe that in my heart, but the facts of the matter lined up, so I had to learn to live with that. The service was wonderful. Everyone respected Pete, regardless of their religious beliefs, and wore Islamic garments.

The Imam allowed people to speak briefly about Pete. I never cried so hard. I knew he was a beautiful person, but I had no idea how beautiful. Pete had helped so many people. My grandmother held me in arms as I laid on her lap and cried my heart out. Guilt crippled me. There is no one else that he had helped more than me and had it not been for me, he would still be here.

Nita showed at the repast to ask about a life insurance policy but went on about her way once I informed her that Pete committed suicide, so all the life insurances were null and void. Sadly, she did not ask about Sharif's wellbeing or even to see him. It did not matter though. I promised Pete I would take care of him and no matter what I was going to keep my word.

I sat in a corner at the repast, just thinking as I looked around. Everyone was fellowshipping and eating and reminiscing about Pete. I had hired a professional decorator, Mrz Gram, to handle the repast and it was nothing short of amazing. I mean she did not miss a single detail. Everything that he was and everything that he stood for was represented in that room. She had definitely outdone herself.

I looked up as a young man came in dressed in all black attire with dark shades. I figured it was someone that Pete knew. I thought I knew everything about this man, but I could not keep up with all his friends I met today. The gentlemen looked around before coming directly to me.

"Hello Ms. Diamond. I am Jahad. You do not know me but I'm a close friend of your late husband. I came to pay my respect and let you know that if you ever need anything, do not hesitate to reach out. That man saved my life from the streets. I owe him all that I am today."

"Wow, for real? That is awesome. May I ask how he saved your life?"

"Ummm....sure. A long time ago, I did something that should have been deemed unforgiveable to someone that he cared deeply about. He could have and should have killed me. Yet, he did not. He made me enroll in a GED program then go to CDL school. He eventually gave me a job at his company. I attended his class every Friday. I had already taken my Shahada but the way he operated as a Muslim man would have made anyone want to get on their Din. I am not going to hold you up though. I just wanted to show love and let you know, I got you." I was sure that I had never seen this man's face before but something about his voice was so familiar.

"Thank you so very much. I appreciate it. Pete was truly an angel on Earth. My phone is dead, but you can write down your number if that's cool." I said handing him a pen. Lilly and Porsha made their way to me as well and took seats beside me. Lilly laid her head on my shoulder and Porsha wrapped her arms around me. I closed my eyes and took in their embrace.

"Here you go." Jahad said. I took the paper from his hand and as soon as our hands touched, I knew exactly who he was. It was not as severe as it used to be, but he still had hands like snakeskin. He turned and headed towards the door. I breathed a heavy sigh of relief once he was gone and calmed myself before I began to hyperventilate.

"What's wrong baby girl?" Lilly asked. I was speechless and my heart was beating fast.

"That was the nigga who kidnapped us when we were in high school and had us hostage in that basement." I said as I thought back to that day. "Devon never paid him. Pete did." I said in total disbelief as I quickly dissected our conversation.

"I am not surprised at all." Porsha said shaking her head. We talked for a little while longer before the time had come for everyone to depart.

I sat in the empty building and said out loud to Pete. "Thank you for teaching me love."

I made my way outside to my car and there, on my windshield laid a single daisy and surely, when I picked it up, it smelled just like Marc Jacobs Daisy.

To Be Continued...

Want To Experience More Good Reads?

Follow:

Instagram: @KiarraWritesLLC

(Short Story Saturdays Are Posted Here)

Tik Tok: @KiarraWritesLLC

Threads: @KiarraWritesLLC

Want To Connect With Kiarra The Don?

Follow:

Instagram: @KiarraTheDon

Tik Tok: @Kiarra.TheDon

Thresads: @KiarraTheDon

Made in the USA
Middletown, DE
27 January 2025

70006596R00150